I AM ALIVE.

There are simple questions. Like, why did the chicken cross the road? Knock, knock. Who's there? Then there are the ones that make no sense. Who ran my dog over yesterday? What kind of person wouldn't even hit the brakes?

Some poet said April is the cruelest month. Now that's something. That stuff can be true without even making sense. And oh, my poor vexed mind. It's everywhere at once. In the fridge stinking with vegetables, under the tires of that awful green car that slammed my Lucky. My mind is like a bad neighborhood: I should not go into it alone.

"[F]ull of clarity and a strange beauty . . . This is a novel that is sure to provoke much thought and debate."

—*School Library Journal*

OTHER PUFFIN BOOKS YOU MAY ENJOY

Stacey Donovan

dive

PUFFIN BOOKS

The author wishes to gratefully acknowledge
Anne Rothkopf, Gilles Lonqueu, and especially
Suzanne Lander for their Rimbaud translations.

PUFFIN BOOKS
Published by the Penguin Group
Penguin Books USA Inc., 375 Hudson Street,
New York, New York 10014, U.S.A.
Penguin Books Ltd, 27 Wrights Lane, London W8 5TZ, England
Penguin Books Australia Ltd, Ringwood, Victoria, Australia
Penguin Books Canada Ltd, 10 Alcorn Avenue, Toronto,
Ontario, Canada M4V 3B2
Penguin Books (N.Z.) Ltd, 182–190 Wairau Road,
Auckland 10, New Zealand

Penguin Books Ltd, Registered Offices: Harmondsworth,
Middlesex, England

First published in the United States of America by Dutton Children's
Books, a division of Penguin Books USA Inc., 1994
Published in Puffin Books, 1996

1 2 3 4 5 6 7 8 9 10

THE LIBRARY OF CONGRESS HAS CATALOGED
THE DUTTON EDITION AS FOLLOWS:
Donovan, Stacey.
Dive/by Stacey Donovan.— 1st ed. p. cm.
Summary: Fifteen-year-old Virginia's world begins to fall apart
when her dog is hit by a car, her father is hospitalized with
a mysterious illness, and her best friend ignores her.
ISBN 0-525-45154-4
[1. Family life—Fiction. 2. Brothers and sisters—Fiction.
3. Friendship—Fiction. 4. Death—Fiction.
5. Lesbians—Fiction. 6. Alcoholism—Fiction. 7. Dogs—Fiction.]
I. Title PZ7.D7236Di 1994
[Fic]—dc20 94-11579 CIP AC

Puffin Books ISBN 0-14-037962-2

Printed in the United States of America

Untalked of and unseen,

in constant memory,

to John

Come hither, man.

SHAKESPEARE

These questions are the simplest in the world.
From the stupid child to the wisest old man,
they are in the soul of every human being.
Without an answer to them, it is impossible,
as I experienced, for life to go on.

TOLSTOY

Contents

dive

Prologue

lucky

My dog was almost dead. Some goon in a green VW Beetle went careening along the road and slammed poor Lucky. Ripped open the dog's leg and drove away. I was chewing a slice of toast in the kitchen when some kids from the bus stop leaned against the doorbell. As I opened the door, I thought Lucky could fly. He leapt from somebody's arms to the step, his whole body in a tremble like it was sixty below zero. Blood spattered everywhere.

As soon as the kids saw me, the one who had carried Lucky, obvious from his ruined shirt, yelled, "The car was green! It was going a hundred miles an hour at least!" Then they all ran away. I couldn't swallow the last bite of toast. It slid across my tongue as my throat closed and I reached for Lucky. It was not even eight o'clock in the morning.

I was barefoot, standing on the cold slate step, my hands deep in Lucky's sleek fur. I lifted him and he groaned wearily, the sound creaking from his small black body. My throat knotted at the sight of the bloody lump. So close to my hand. Don't hurt him. Bits of skin swung in clumps and pieces from his leg. The air somersaulted in a frantic rush. Oh—my breath. I wondered what to do.

Up the driveway rolled a big gold Cadillac. A gray-haired man pushed the door open. "How's the dog?" he called.
I couldn't say, not even if I'd wanted to.
"I saw what happened," he said. His eyes were as bright as flashlights.
I still couldn't swallow.
"Is anybody home?"
For an instant it felt like he had come to the house to sell something—flashlights? In another instant I real-

ized everybody in my family was on their way somewhere else, nowhere I could reach them. The man took a few quiet steps toward me. When I looked down, I saw loafers on his feet.

"They're gone," I said, my chin lightly brushing the moaning Lucky's head. My arms held him so that he rested, in a cradled way, against the soft flesh of my inner elbows.

"I can take you to the vet. What vet do you go to?"

"The closest one," I said. Lucky's regular vet was miles away, but there was a new one in town.

I was afraid to move. My poor groaning dog. His endless, seeping blood. I stepped to the driveway. Lucky writhed in my arms.

"But you . . . you're not wearing any shoes," the man said.

"It doesn't matter."

And for a moment I wondered if this was who had hit Lucky. A gold Cadillac? Figures, the one moment in my life it would be useful to have a family, I don't.

The car owner gunned the engine, the fingers of one hand tapping his stomach as if something alive was there. "Now which way do we go?"

'Just before the train station, on the right. You can take the back way." I wished he would steer with both hands.

"The back way? I don't live around here."

"Can you get to town?" I asked. "Make a left here, and another at the stop sign down the road." Lucky panted.

He nodded, then shook his head. "I was a few hundred yards behind. The absolute gall of people is hard to believe; it's simply beyond me."

"You couldn't see the driver?"

"Only the car, one of those old Bugs, you know which one I mean? A real jalopy. I didn't even see any brake lights."

"Thank you" was the last thing I said, other than giving him simple directions to the new office complex I'd passed on my way to school. Be polite, my mind said. Don't talk to strangers.

A black CLOSED *sign hung below Dr. Wheatie's name in an otherwise empty window. The place was so new there wasn't even a curtain. Dr. Wheatie? I kicked the door anyway, since my hands held Lucky, until the vet himself appeared, shrugging into a white lab coat. The stranger was still behind me, wiping at the red mess on his beige deep-dish car seat. My jeans were soaked, and brown foam oozed from Lucky's jaws. The vet's sleepy eyelids lifted with surprise. I opened my mouth, but my voice didn't follow.*

"This way—let's hurry now." We followed Dr. Wheatie through the office into the examination room, the stiff

bottom of his coat flapping. The new stainless steel of
the heavy table was like a spotlight. Its brightness hurt
my eyes as I bent over with Lucky, as I said unending
stupid stuff, like "Hey boy. My boy boy baby." Just to
say something. For my dog's sake.

The vet leaned over too. Lucky was panting like he'd
run a big race. Dr. Wheatie tried not to tug at the pieces
that were once his leg, and I tried not to let Lucky bite
the vet, though his attempts lacked steam, and eventually his most menacing growl became a whimper. I felt
my face drain each time Lucky yelped. What happens to
the heart when it forgets to beat? Can it catch up later
or is the moment lost forever?

The car owner appeared, wincing in the background,
his eyes dim. The vet finally said Lucky needed an operation and turned to the stranger. The air, so still with
tension, stank.
"No, no, not me. Not related. I just drove her here," the
Cadillac owner said, both hands up like he surren-
dered. Dr. Wheatie nodded and looked at me. His eyes
were blue. "You're underage. I'll need your parents'
permission—and soon." He started to scratch behind
the dog's ears. Lucky let him.

I grabbed the phone behind the table. I remembered my
mother's unfamiliar work number without a thought,
which to me was a feat as good as lifting a car with

one superhuman hand. I was yelling "Hello" into the phone when she answered, but then my voice became strangled. All I could get out was a meager "Lucky . . ." My throat tumbled into a sob. I couldn't help it.

The vet's hand left mine, the one that still held my dog's trembling collarbone. I hadn't been aware of his hand until he removed it. If I had been, I would've moved my own hand sooner. Don't touch me. What was no longer there had more impact once it was gone. That was something. Like memory was sturdier than reality. I closed my eyes to stop the tears in front of everybody.

He reached for the phone. I must've missed a few words. ". . . Vital signs good. The hind leg is badly torn, probably fractured. . . . It could be some time . . . hard to say . . . maybe five hundred dollars. Yes . . . that would be the end of it." Dr. Wheatie hung up. What happened to 'Good-bye'?

The vet's shoulders stiffened as he walked, no, shuffled, across the room. A drawer opened and Dr. Wheatie removed a syringe, which proceeded to roll on the desk top until he grabbed it. He shut the drawer and took a small bottle of some clear stuff from the back of a shelf overhead. The vet's shoulders were like rocks. He didn't look at me. Is it possible to climb out of one moment into the next? I wanted to. Being in that room was like being inside a cannon.

I held Lucky tighter. He growled as Dr. Wheatie looked at him, as he came toward us with a frown on his face. "What's his name?" said the vet. Why did he sound that way, like something stood on top of his voice, weighing it down?
"Lucky."

"So it's Lucky." Dr. Wheatie looked at the Cadillac owner. There was something crushing the air. They stared at each other. Like I wasn't really there. Like it wasn't my dog and I wasn't covered with blood, standing between them in this room. No, no, not my cold feet on that cement floor sensing the stupid this-is-not-as-serious-as-it-looks moment adults like to pull. Sure, life's a dream. Anybody home?

"Hey," I said, "what's going on?" Was that my voice? Dr. Wheatie coughed, which allowed his shoulders to return to the position they normally occupy on a body, rather than crowding his ears. "You've got to hold Lucky," he said, "and I . . . pretty soon . . . he won't feel anything."
The stuff in his hand clattered onto the shining table. I saw his narrow, tentative fingers. His smooth hands. Dr. Wheatie was new at this.

"What are you doing?" I asked. Lucky flinched.

"The dog's going to sleep." The vet tried to smile. Instead, his mouth looked like a cracked rock. "I mean . . . I'm sorry."

"Then what?" Sorry to interrupt. Lucky began groaning again.

"Then . . . your mother . . . I have no choice. We'll let him go."

"Let him go? Like what, off to heaven?" I think I was loud. Nobody spoke. Lucky didn't move. I gathered him more snugly in my arms.

"Now, now. Can't there be another way out of this?" said the Cadillac owner, his absurd hands waving through the air. Where was he from, anyway?

The vet just looked at the stranger's hands.

"She won't pay? Fine. I can pay," I said. I noticed my feet were cold. How dumb. "If you, if you would let me work for you—animals love me." I stopped. "Please."

The vet's hand rubbed his chin. "Well, there's a thought." And then he really smiled. His teeth were white as snow. "I need help. Now let's see if we can get this poor guy out of pain. We'll need X rays first thing. Good!"

My feet froze. "Let's see," I said. Had I truly spoken? A part of me felt like I wasn't really alive. But I could taste it, the question was so bitter.

Who hit my dog?

unlucky

I am alive. At fifteen, I find myself staring at the shelves
of food in the refrigerator. What, I'd like to know, are
celery hearts?

There are simple questions. Like, why did the chicken
cross the road? Knock, knock. Who's there? Then there
are the ones that make no sense. Who ran my dog over

yesterday? What kind of person wouldn't even hit the brakes?

Some poet said April is the cruelest month. Now that's something. That stuff can be true without even making sense. And oh, my poor vexed mind. It's everywhere at once. In the fridge stinking with vegetables, under the tires of that awful green car that slammed my Lucky. My mind is like a bad neighborhood: I should not go into it alone.

No, life doesn't make sense.

But I am alive anyway. I live in the suburbs, land of car rides to the Dairy Barn. Around here, nobody ever walks. Everybody does walk to the end of the driveway to get the mail, and now that it's the end of April, everyone mows the lawn so early in the morning it's like a contest to see who can start first. Everyone does the same thing, yet everybody looks at everyone else in a suspicious way. A northeastern suburban existence. *Sub* means "under." Under life. So where are we?

I live in a big gray house. No matter how big, the sorry truth is that the house is inescapably small. There's always somebody around to bother me, or somebody's forgotten socks to remind me that they were around. There's not a house big enough in the world to hold us,

I'd say, if anyone asked. People call the place lovely.
But what is lovely? We have a lawn that looks like it
just rolled out of a truck.

In my youth I wondered how the JOHNNY'S PERFECT
LAWN trucks that roamed the neighborhood could roll
great, sprawling lawns out of them. I decided the bigger
trucks must arrive in the middle of the night, so we are
dizzedly surprised when we wake up and look through
our windows at our new, perfect lawn. Dizzedly. Our
lives are complete. That's a good one.

When I mentioned this to Edward, my brother, he said
I was an idiot. As if he's in any way smart. I admit it
was dumb of me to let down my guard like that. When
people are a few years older, they sometimes think
they know everything. He's seventeen

Look who's talking, I say. Edward, aka the Wad, received his eloquent surname in recognition of his ability to jam entire hamburgers into his barbaric mouth.
Now that's lovely. My dad started calling him Wad,
and it stuck because it fits. I'm V. Victory comes
to mind, since I have actually survived life with my
brother. I like to remember that I was much younger
when I had the lawn thoughts.

Certainly younger than my sister, Baby Teeth, who is
eight. Hers is not a nickname, but a fact. Not one loose

tooth in all these years. Not even a single Tooth Fairy sighting. Though her dental development may be lax, Baby Teeth is an otherwise progressive kid. Her favorite activity this year is to drop by other people's houses. People she doesn't know. Generally she will call home before dinner to say where she is, not that she's ever actually been invited anywhere. Then somebody has to collect her. Usually it's me.

I've met many people because of Baby Teeth. Though she has a lot to say after her visits, like whether or not there is any baloney in someone's fridge or if a certain stranger wears slippers, she will not disclose why she does it. My mother grinds her teeth when the phone rings. Otherwise, we've accepted it. Perhaps our house is too small for Baby Teeth as well.

At least the lawn is big enough. Old apple trees surround one side of the house. Trees that were here, no doubt, long before the house was built. Before any happy family moved in.

Now that it's spring, baby rabbits wobble beneath the trees every time I look outside. They somersault in midair and end up facing the direction they were hopping from, all shocked, like they don't know how they landed there. I guess they don't. How much can any living thing know that's only been around for a few short weeks? It makes me wonder how much I knew when I was a tiny, wobbling baby. I admit I feel pretty confused now. I have hazel eyes. They go green when I cry.

They're still green today. Can my eyes have their own memories? It was yesterday I wept, the reverberations of a car crashing a hundred miles an hour, crashing into my bones. Vast amounts of blood dry incredibly fast, I discovered. Then it's sticky, like glue. The discovery twisted like glue in my stomach as I peeled off my jeans, after the extemely kind stranger from Wyoming, Bertrand Utley, dropped Lucky and me back home.

Maybe my eyes know more than I do today. Maybe they're preparing for what's next. It seems yesterday was just a tipoff to the fact that life has some unspoken and probably incomprehensible plans of its own. Because today, after I arrived home from school, my parents drove off in our car with my dad's brown leather suitcase tossed in the backseat. But it's not a vacation. My dad's on the way to the hospital. And what's wrong with him? Nobody knows.

I wish I could just shut my eyes. But even when they're closed, I can still see it. Now there's something else that doesn't make sense but is true. In my guts I can see it: the beginning of the Dunn downhill slide.

| | |

So my eyes are open, and I stare into the yellow fridge, which always smells like egg salad though there's never any of that, looking for something delectable that will entice Lucky to eat. In the den, Baby Teeth is keeping him company as I search. Lucky hasn't eaten since yesterday's breakfast, not even a spoonful of chocolate ice cream or a busted-up potato chip, his favorites. Mine too.

Dr. Wheatie said a lack of appetite wouldn't be unusual. It takes time to recover from shock. Not to mention Lucky's inability to walk. The cast on his left leg starts above the ankle and ends at the hip. When we try to walk again tomorrow, we'll just pretend it's natural to hobble like we've only got three legs. His paw was miraculously unharmed, or else we wouldn't be pretending. Maybe there *is* something in a name.

But celery hearts? Really.

We've had Lucky since I was seven. He was the one at the shelter hiding at the back of the kennel. Lucky, according to his chart, was already a year old. So in dog years, he's almost retired now. Sixty-three.
"He's the one," I said, as the small black shadow in the corner watched with unblinking eyes.
"What about a shepherd? Do they have any labradors?" my mother asked. "Shepherds are such good watchdogs. The Millers' never shuts up."

"Him."

"She wants a mutt." My father laughed. It was his idea to get a dog. Edward was at baseball practice. We were going to surprise him.

"A crazy mutt," my mother said. She didn't laugh.

"I'd say he was a pretty lucky dog." That was my dad.

"Lucky," I said, "let's go, boy."

Who in the world but a crazy mutt would follow me everywhere I go?

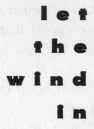

let the wind in

A bowl of luscious vanilla pudding might make any dog hungry. This is my impression as I carry one into the den, low-ash dog biscuits filling my other hand, enough to please a sudden canine appetite. I find Baby Teeth kneeling on the carpet next to the red couch, singing to Lucky. What a sweet kid. Some old tune about sunshine and life, and really she's crooning so well that Lucky, all stretched out on top of some throw pillows like a king, can't keep his eyes open.

I silently edge myself into one of the red easy chairs, so as not to interrupt. I look out the window at the birds. The lawn is so full of them, the birds seem to grow out of the ground. I feed them when I can, which means I have to steal some bread and nuts when my mother isn't around. Otherwise my mother's vocal cords resonate with loud, nasty words.

Birds, more than most other beasts, are high on her hit list. Because they miscalculate and dump turds on her car—isn't that tragic? Feeding them just invites trouble, she claims. How my parents got together I'll never know. My dad loves animals.

But at least I can feed the birds. So what if I feel like a criminal when I do? The sensation is not terrible— the suspense makes my heart pound. In the end it may be a positive cardiovascular exercise. Criminal activity also smells good—it fills the air. Danger, I think, smells like the glob of leftover hot chocolate at the bottom of the cup, black and slightly burnt.

At night there's a riot at the back of the house. It's the raccoons, rolling the garbage cans around like bowling balls. I'm seriously not allowed to feed *them* at all.

My mother has mentioned, in her deadpan way, that "Food is not what they need. Maybe poison." My mother can be very funny, especially when she's not trying. I've wondered if that poison crack was really confined to the raccoons. Or am I just unfathomably paranoid?

"Spiders are stronger than steel," Baby Teeth says. I turn my gaze from the birds to my sister's clear brown eyes. Baby Teeth makes this kind of statement when she wants to avoid something. One small hand rests on Lucky's tail.

"Who told you that?" I say.

"Mr. Connor."

Mr. Connor is my best friend Eileen's dad. "Yup. Better parachutes, bulletproof vests, and clubs, clubs . . . *golf* clubs." She sits back and rubs her bare knees through the holes in her jeans.

"You mean spiders are making golf clubs now? Sometimes you can't believe everything people tell you."

She tugs at some loose threads on her pants. "Oh, Virginia, I'm talking about spider *silk*. It was on PBS."

"Right, thoughtless of me. Look how Lucky liked your singing." Lucky's tongue droops from his jaw as he sleeps.

"I know. That song always puts me to sleep," she says. "I just do it usually without making noise." A smile widens her face. "Well, think about Mr. Connor picking his nose. I saw him; don't tell me I can't believe it." Baby Teeth is also very attentive to any disgusting personal habits people might have.

"Wouldn't dream of it." She hasn't been over there often enough—but I have. Mr. Connor cuts the foulest air known to man. "Baby Teeth," I say softly, "Dad's going to be okay—he just went in for some tests. There's no reason to worry."

"How do you know?" She stares at me.

I have to remember I'm talking to a person who sleeps with her eyes open. That's really true. I used to think it meant that she never actually slept—that she was only pretending. But it's a matter of eyelids, is all. Baby Teeth's won't stay shut. "Well, Edward's not around, is he? Don't you think if something big and terrible were happening, he would be here?"

Now her eyes are on Lucky's cast. Baby Teeth thinks before she speaks, something I like about her. "Well, yeah," she finally says. "I guess so."

I am such a good liar.

Where is my brother? We've got a damaged dog and a hospital-bound father, so where is he? Probably unconscious somewhere, a common occurrence, or doing some rock climbing inside his head.

| | |

Edwad has his own room on the first floor for no other reason than he's the boy. Aside from being slept in, his room is generally empty because Wadnod is never home. Homework is an absent word in my brother's vocabulary anyway. Neanderthals were not known to be big scholars, so I'm not surprised.

I assume he feels secure sleeping close to his car, which is parked outside his window. For Wadbrain's prized possession, it's a toss-up between the old Plymouth rust heap that my dad bought him when Wadstain got his driver's permit last year and his shoulder-length ponytailed hair. He's got four different conditioners in his bathroom. Is it the end, or the stifling beginning, of obsession? Va va va voom.

Baby Teeth and I share a room all the way at the end of the house on the second floor, which is how I've become aware of her sleeping patterns. Who knows how much I've said to that sleeping body because her eyes were staring at me? Our room has a door that's curved on top like a half moon. It's really unusual. I like unusual stuff. I like the door shut. Baby Teeth prefers it open. "Let the wind in," she says. What wind? I wonder if she means that some moments are so still, especially in *this* house, it seems like they vanish before they really even exist. But I don't want to ask—she's already told me that some questions of mine scare her.

My brother says that Baby Teeth's a real piece of work.
It is, incredibly, a thought I can agree with. She's also
hopelessly cute, with light brown hair that curls around
her shoulders and highlights her unquestionable dimples. Nobody can resist her. I suppose that's why people
let her follow them around in their houses, instead of
calling the police or somebody like me right away to
come and get her.

Wadhead ignores me and Eileen when he sees us
around town, as if I'm not his sister, who eats dinner
with him every night. When he shows up, that is. Like
I'm this perfectly invisible stranger he couldn't see even
if he wanted to. "Virginia," I will say when he stares
through me with bloodshot eyes in that hunched, vul-
turelike way of his, as he chews his potatoes. Oh, I am
weak-kneed with fear. "My name is Virginia and I
exist."
"You don't exist," he will say.

"Over a million species of insects exist; do you know
that?" Baby Teeth will say.
"No crap," my brother's porkchop-chewing mouth might
reply. Not even the Wadness can resist her.
"Insects rule," she'll announce. "You just watch." And
as she explains, her silverware might land on the floor,
since her hands are always busy when she talks. The
word is not *clumsy*, but *preoccupied*, I think. She tends
to knock stuff over.

। । ।

Lucky barks with high-pitched fervor when that happens. Because all stray morsels, as unspoken dog law would have it, are his. He's smart enough to sit at Baby Teeth's heels at dinner. Until yesterday, anyhow. Sometimes I don't know who I feel closer to.

**a r e
y o u
t a l k i n g
t o
m e ?**

The sky is immense in April. Beneath it, anything seems possible. Baby Teeth is asleep next to Lucky. Might as well do some homework—all reading. Yes! Any day without math is a good one. It's ten pages of Shakespeare for English and a chapter of some supposedly well-spun noise called *The Varieties of Religious Experience* for my elective, Western philosophy. But first, some pudding. Save it for the dog, tubby.

To begin with, how can *things so insecure as
the successful experiences of this world afford a
stable anchorage? A chain is no stronger than
its weakest link, and life is after all a chain. In
the healthiest and most prosperous existence,
how many links of illness, danger, and disaster
are always interposed?*

Somebody help me, please. What *I* read was: Life is a
chain. How many links of illness, danger, and disaster
are interposed? The answer to that, in this house, is
one of each. Except for the dangerous element, who
is elsewhere, and possibly reapplying lipstick at this
moment.

"Is Dad home?"
Oh, there's the vulture in the doorway. I didn't hear
him come in. That means my brother's car must be
running unnaturally well. Usually the Plymouth rum-
bles up the driveway. They'd like it to "purr," Wadstain
and my dad, which is why they are often found, hands
under its hood, on weekend mornings. Wadnod is wearing a faded army jacket and mud-stained jeans. Very
cool. It looks like he's been slam-dancing with the
ground. "No stronger than its weakest link."
"Are you talking to me?" I say.

| | |

"Nah, it's the chair I figure I'll hear from." His dark brown ponytail flops around. "I don't got time for this, you know. So is he or not?"

I notice his earlobes turning red, so I relent. "They're not home yet." My chin tilts toward the couch's dozing lumps. "Be quiet."

"Well, that's all you gotta say, you know." He keeps his voice down, which is phenomenal, then follows with his classic vulture face, cheeks all sucked in, lips curled. Oh, I am stunned with terror. The final say is always my brother's, whether it's with his sneer or impressive truck-driver vocabulary. I really wonder what the girls see in him. He's built like a scarecrow under all those baggy clothes, so it must be the car. Some females are truly desperate.

"Is that right?" I say. "And 'hello' is probably something you could manage." Screw him.

"Oh yeah? Well, I don't got time for small talk."

I have nothing else to say. I look back at my book. The chapter is appropriately called "The Sick Soul." 'How many links . . . ?' Really.

"Yeah, I'm busy. . . ."

Yeah, he looks busy. Why is he telling me the same nothing thing twice? The Wad doesn't seem to remember he never speaks to me. I realize my dad's hospital trip has my brother really rattled, and I'm uncomfortable. Change the subject. "Did the paper come?"

"Huh?"

"Hi, Edward." Baby Teeth is awake.

"The newspaper."

"I suppose it's out there." He nods at Baby Teeth.

Lucky yawns. I'll carry him outside, see if the grass reminds him of his former life. Then maybe his appetite will come back. Dr. Wheatie showed me how to lift him, both arms under the stomach. The cradle again.

"At least say hello to the dog, will you?"

"Time for a run, huh, Pegleg?"

We all crack up. It's so unexpected, my face hurts. With their idiotic grins, my siblings don't even look like the same people.

The back door slams.

"They're home!" Baby Teeth is gone. Out the den, through the living room, the hall with its fake palm tree, into the kitchen. I hear only the clack of high heels on the kitchen's yellow linoleum floor. My mother. Where's Dad? I look at my brother. He's chewing the tip of his filthy thumb.

"Huh," he says.

"Right." 'How *can* things so insecure as the successful experiences of this world afford a stable anchorage?' I'm beginning to understand. My brother is going. I hear Baby Teeth asking my mother questions in the kitchen.

"Edward?" I say. Who?

"Yeah."

"Ever read any James?"

"James who?"

I'll take the dog out. Get some air. Why not? He's in my arms. We'll use the front door. William, William James.

It seemed like the flu last week. So my dad kept sleeping. But nobody else around here caught it, which is unusual. After three days, my dad wasn't better and stopped eating. He had gone back to the office last Thursday anyway, because he is a stubborn mule, according to my mother. When he came home that night, he was just a paler and skinnier version of himself. He went to bed.

The next morning he looked even worse and finally agreed to go with my mother to the doctor, who at first also thought it was the flu. And then maybe more than the flu. The symptoms of mononucleosis—terrible chills and pains, complete exhaustion, muscle cramping—were the stuff my dad felt, and so Dr. Sweeney wanted to have some blood work done.

Dad came home from Dr. Sweeney's and slept all weekend. He ate a full dinner on Sunday, his first entire

meal in days, and claimed he felt better. But he was
gray. Even his lips.

Yesterday, which was Monday, he went back to work.
Because he's a fool, said my mother. Was that yesterday? Yes, as I dropped some six-grain bread into
the toaster slots. I hadn't even put my socks on yet.
Everybody had left. Then the doorbell rang . . .
and Lucky . . .

And today, Dad stayed home again. They waited. . . .
The mono test was negative. Off to the hospital they
went. Okay, it's not mono. So what is it?

Lucky eyes the grass. He sniffs, attempts to lift his
leg. He groans because he can't. I groan. Anyway,
he can pee. Good. That's my boy. I carry him around
the side of the house. I see my mother through
the kitchen window. Her mouth is moving. Of course
I can't hear the words. I wait. Her hand lifts the
glass to her lips. A wicked gulp. Unparalleled,
really. So much can happen in so little liquid. But
under an April sky anything is possible. Once she
swallows, the edge of her mood softens. It's okay to
go in.

"They want to keep him overnight," she says as I shut
the kitchen door with my foot, Lucky in my arms. She

has a gift for stating the obvious and lying about everything else. My mother wanted to kill my dog. She made *that* clear enough with no trouble. So why not say everything she knows about Dad? The irritation drags along my tongue like a rusty chain. I can taste it. I hate my mother.

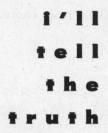

i'll tell the truth

Sometimes it's better not to say a word. Raisinets come to mind.

It was my mother who came downstairs in a hurry last Friday morning, before we left for school, to telephone the doctor. I remember another emergency call when Baby Teeth wedged several Raisinets up her preschool nose. She had just turned three. Eventually the chocolate melted and she was able to blow them out, unscathed.

Morning has never been my mother's chosen time of day. She's just not herself. Hell, the day didn't start until the 5:00 P.M. ice cubes sent cold music into her waiting glass. Well, on Friday morning her hands shook so badly that to hit the buttons on the phone she had to put the receiver on the kitchen table because she had already dropped it twice.

Whoever answered must've said the doctor was busy or something because my mother said, "So sorry to burst that bubble!" She slammed the phone down, stomped upstairs, and they left the house immediately. My dad was still in his pajamas, too, which was just awful. I mean, picture it. A grown man in his blue plaids whisked away to the doctor. Like a cartoon but the opposite of funny.

The image of those electronic chairs that glide up and down the stairs came stupidly into my head. I had seen the commercial about a thousand times on late-night television. My dad's face was all puffy and yellow beside his mouth. Around him, the air was green. Who cares if it's possible or not; it's true. It took him forever to come down the stairs, even with my mother and EdWad supporting him under his armpits. My brother's face was the color of an old plum.

I almost dropped my bowl of cereal when I saw them. I looked over at Baby Teeth. Can eyes rumble? Hers were. What is she so afraid of? Does she think Dad is going to *die* or something? I thought. But I would never have said that. And why not is because I wasn't sure that those thoughts weren't coming from the inside of my own head. It's better not to say a word sometimes.

We were in the living room. Baby Teeth had followed me in because she wanted the rest of my Banana Nut Crunch cereal. She could easily have made herself ten bowls, but that was not the point. She was after mine, the milk just wetting, not drowning, the stuff so it still crunched.

"We're going to Dr. Sweeney. Don't miss the bus," my mother said. Wadnod loped away, mumbling "Good luck," I think. When the door closed behind them, I walked over to Baby Teeth.
"I can't eat it all." I handed her my cereal. The smell of bananas filled the air between us.
She took it.

There are, however, occasions when it is crucial to say stuff out loud. This is true in friendship. Eileen Connor and I have been best friends forever. We've been in the same grade since kindergarten and always sit near each other in any classes we share because of our last names—Connor and Dunn. And we're both Irish. All somebody has to do is see her red bush of hair hovering above the street like a big cloud to see how Irish Eileen is.

It wasn't always a bush. Not many Irish people have natural hair bushes, I suspect. But she needed a change a few months ago. Before the cut, her hair looked like a piece of discolored corn attached to the back of her head. Because it was utterly impossible for Eileen to get a comb through the heap when it got loose, she held it captive with a barrette.

I convinced her to have her hair permed and cut because she became so depressed about it. She wouldn't talk about anything else once she was obsessed, and that became pretty dull. "Corncob," I simply said, "it's a mess. Cut it off."

I'm Black Irish. I've got the dark wavy hair, with just a shadow of chestnut in it. They call us Black Irish because the Spanish fleets invaded Ireland centuries ago and pillaged the towns and raped the women. So some Irish are freckled and red-haired, and some are pale and black-haired, because of the Spanish. I guess I must have old Spanish blood in me too. Perhaps this accounts for some of my bad temper. What bad temper? Did my mother say that? Maybe it's just the feeling she's out to get me. Unfathomably paranoid? Who knows. *Pillage* is a great word, though. Pillage, loot, and plunder.

I think I'll call Eileen right now. Maybe we can get out of the house for a while. She lives just around the corner, so she's number 2 on the phone's memory. There is no number 1, which is perplexing. The memory only runs numbers 2 through 9. Why? Stuff without reasons always annoys me.

"What are you doing?" I say.
"Oh, hi. Well, since it's you, I'll tell the truth. I'm sitting here holding my breath, but every so often I have to gasp because I'm worried about killing off some of the brain cells I might need to get my homework done. . . . Not that this material on metamorphic rocks is greatly challenging, mind you, but I try. But, V, I have this oozing feeling that my face will turn blue—and stay that way. I mean, now and happily ever after. Can you imagine?"

Eileen's elective this semester is geology. "Did you say metamorphic rocks? What do they do? Change into people? Let's see if I can name one. . . . How about Loretta Getz, metamorphosed pebble-brain?"
"Sedimentary, my dear Watson." Eileen laughs.

"So what was it today?" I am, as usual, referring to her father's 'intestinal complications.'

"My guess is something from the bottom of the sea. You'd think he'd at least confine himself to one room instead of spreading it around everywhere so other people die of the fumes. Maybe I could go on TV, and we could unearth some *cure*. What do you think, V? 'Daughter gulps for air—story at four.' "

"It's an idea—let's make a list of all the talk shows. Can you get out for a while?"

Eileen hesitates. "I think so. Maybe a little race-walk before dinner, okay? Some *fresh air*. See you in ten."

Eileen is taller than most guys, and to her horror, just as flat-chested. Her features are as sharp as her manner—the long, straight nose, the firm, determined mouth. Only her eyes, more gray than a sky blue, are soft. This combination of qualities has made her popular. The new cloud of hair helps even more.

I've always admired that sharpness of hers. Eileen knows what she thinks about something, it seems, without even thinking. I'm the opposite. If we see a whodunit, and it's any *good*, it's not until later I can really decide how all the parts of the movie fit together. My mind seems to like rewinding stuff before it finds any answers, whereas Eileen's operates in fast forward.

Ten minutes into a film, she'll blurt out who the murderer is—and she's usually right.

Today, we decide to walk through the new development, called Sagamore, which is close by.

"How's Lucky, poor little creature?"

"Still a wreck. He won't eat."

"Well, you know, I'm surprised you left the house at all."

"I know he'll be there when I get back. Baby Teeth's watching him. My dad's staying at the hospital."

"Wow, he is? For how long?"

"I don't know. Tests."

"Oh, horrible. V, that's bad, or what?"

"I don't know either." I shrug on purpose. I want to ignore how my heart stops as I say those words. "Whatever it is, it's not good."

We used to ride sleds here when we were kids, but all the sledding hills were destroyed to make room for these houses. It's all flat now, the most pitiful strands of grass inching out of the brown, steamrolled ground.

Eileen does the deep-knee bends we are required to do at the beginning of gym three times a week. "What, *really*, are these good for, I'd like to know? I mean, in what context in my actual life will I perform this move?"

"Knees are your friends, don't forget. So what's for dinner?" I say. I want to lighten things up.

"What did I do to deserve this?" She stretches as she stands and her voice fills this empty place. "Spaghetti with *clam* sauce. There's no possible relief anywhere in this horrible world."

"Well, at least there's a theme here, some *consistency*, this *underwater* kind of thing," I say.

We laugh.

We don't race-walk. We are, in fact, walking as slowly as old ladies. This place is awful. We look around, staring, speechless, at the houses. They forgot something important when they built this place: imagination. Just what we need—a new place that's more lifeless than the one we already live in. Every house we pass could be the one before. House after house, porch, blacktop driveway. Identical. Since there are no people around, it's also completely still.

"I wonder who'll move in," Eileen finally says.

"Robots. Astronauts, maybe. Sheep."

"Let's change the subject," she says, and her voice changes too, into something hard, impatient.

"Okay. Well, I heard something—it's a game, sort of. There are four questions. Ready?"

She only nods, glances at her watch.

We're standing in the middle of a new black road.

"What's your favorite mammal?"

"Does that include frogs?" she says.

"Frogs are amphibians."

"So? You didn't say there were rules." The hard edge
of her tone jumps into her eyes as they become bright.

"Eileen, this is a *game*. Don't go serious on me here."
What's wrong? I want to say, but I don't—I don't like
that new voice of hers. "Okay, we'll count frogs, since
they're alive. So frogs?"

"No, fish are my favorite."

"Okay then, fish." I feel like I'm talking to someone
else. Fish?

"Why?"

She's staring at me. Metamorphic rocks, did she say?

"Well, don't you want to know what *kind* of fish?"

"Sure." It's like somebody else has come along and
usurped my friend's body. I struggle to keep my voice
regular. "What kind?"

"Goldfish!"

"Uh huh. . . . Why's that?"

"Is this the game? Because they're not going to end up
dead on some hook. Virginia, did you ever see a goldfish that wasn't in a bowl? They're completely *safe*."

I don't think it's the ideal moment to mention that
goldfish are actually carp. Carp are freshwater fish that
do not always end up trapped in aquariums. I just
say, "I guess so."

"And they're so pretty."

"Same color as your hair."

"Nice attitude, V. I thought this was a *game*."

"That was a *compliment*." It's like there are now two people inside her—the one I know, and this twisted, sarcastic one who is possessing her. I can't stand it anymore. "It's like there's something eating at your brain, Eileen. *What* is it?"

"Nothing, just nothing, *all right?* Is that the end of the game? So let's get out of here."

I follow. "No." And no, it's not all right. "What's your favorite color?"

"You don't *know?*" She sighs. "Oh, I don't know, there's too many." Eileen walks faster. I guess we're race-walking now.

"Body of water?" Something has to give. I know what will happen—finally she'll explode and tell me everything.

"What?"

"Your favorite." Your *problem*, I think.

"Oh . . . a stream, I guess. Why? Because it's gentle, doesn't go very far. Anything else?"

I laugh before I can stop. She can't imagine what she's *admitting*, because she doesn't know what the questions mean.

"What's so funny?"

"You have to wait. Last one: You're in a white room with a curved ceiling. No windows. No doors. How do you feel?"

"How do I *feel?* Like I'm suffocating, the same experience I'm having with these questions. Anyone ever tell you you're a real *pain?*"

I blink. A Baby Teeth remark enters my mind: Let the wind in. Even though we're outside, surrounded only by space, the air seems to have vanished. I mean the air *inside* too. Eileen might as well have socked me, the way my stomach feels, clobbered and hollow. That was so unbelievably *mean*, and why? I can only look at Eileen. The back of her, anyway, since she's already several steps ahead.

Instead of turning around to look at me, Eileen eyes her watch. "I really have to go, right now." She walks faster.

My feet feel numb, like they're asleep—I can't go that fast. "Wait." What's going on? She's possessed.

"So hurry up, I gotta get home. Nothing!"

"You don't eat dinner this early. It can't even be six o'clock." I try to catch up, but then I realize I don't want to.

"If you must know, I'm expecting a phone call, and would you please stop asking so many questions?"

A phone call? Something's wrong, but she's not telling me what. This is not like Eileen—she tells me everything. The fact that she's not is burning the edges of my eyes. What's wrong with me? What's wrong with *her?* "From who?" I finally ask.

| | |

But she doesn't answer. I want to forget everything else and tell her what the game really means, that the first answer is supposedly who she *really is*, and the second, what somebody *shows* to the world instead. The third one is how somebody feels about *sex*, and the last, about *death*. Look at all the stuff you're missing about yourself, I want to yell. Don't you want to know?

But when I open my mouth, no sound follows. Like yesterday when we stood outside the vet's. My new mode of expression. I shut my mouth. Out of the silence looms an unusual thought. It blurs the street below my feet. As I walk behind her, she begins to resemble someone I barely know. With my eyes all out of focus, she even walks like a stranger. Not a word.

vertigo

The sky slants. Before dusk, it hurts my eyes. Soon it will be completely dark. I'm walking home. Nothing exists but my breath. I know this feeling. Usually it comes when something unexpected and momentously awful is about to happen, which doesn't make sense now. I'm just going home.

I I I

I had the feeling big in seventh grade, when someone brought a message from the principal's office into my social studies class one day. The note said my mother wanted me to go directly home after school. It was obvious that something was disastrously wrong, since I'd never received a note from my mother—especially not in school. Even though I knew it was something dreadful, I felt special.

That day, as I waited for school to end, I watched myself do what everybody else did. I opened and shut my desk, reached for my books, and since my hands had become unnaturally heavy as I placed pencil tip to page, I kept breaking the black point when I was writing down the populations of Far Eastern countries. So I was sharpening my pencils with my blue whale-shaped sharpener too. I watched myself behave as if nothing was wrong, but what really happened is that a part of me lifted out of my chair and rose to the ceiling of the room and floated there, watching the whole scene. And the me that was left behind in the chair had this gruesome crawling feeling beneath my skin.

The feeling is called anxiety, but I didn't know that then. That was three years ago. Nobody around my neighborhood ever called feelings by names. Only books did. I attached the word to the feeling when I read Dostoyevsky's *Crime and Punishment*. It's an old book of my dad's. Raskolnikov, the main character, was full of anxiety. Obviously, this was because he had killed somebody. Books have saved my life, or stopped me from thinking I'm purely crazy anyway.

So I did go directly home after school, but not before I found Baby Teeth. She was telling everybody on the bus line that she had a note and should be able to get on first. We rode home together on my bike. I wanted to put her on the seat, but riding on the handlebars was a big deal for her when she was in first grade, so I let her. The ride was smooth. Even though it was February and unbearably cold, she didn't complain. The tears just froze on her face. "Are you crying?" I asked when we stopped and I brushed her hair away from her eyes, but she wouldn't answer. Just offered me her wet-mittened hand, which I held until we were well inside the house. Poor kid, she was scared. And maybe that's what the feeling in my throat was, like a burst of wind through a pile of leaves.

We found my mother, who was usually hovering around the kitchen when we returned from school, sitting in the den with the Wad. The telephone was poised on the arm of her chair. The den walls are made of wood, and heavy drapes edge the windows, so it can be very dark in there at any hour, and it was that day. The drapes had been pulled across the windows. The bronze table lamp was lit, which was unnatural, since it was afternoon. It was eerie.

My brother was sitting on the couch staring into the empty fireplace. Baby Teeth let go of my hand. She rammed herself against my mother's legs, who, instead of grabbing her, which would've been a natural mother move to make, just kept her eyes on the telephone. I walked over and took Baby Teeth's wet mittens off. There were white ducks on them.

"What's wrong?" I finally asked. All I could hear was my own breath.

"Pop died," my mother said. Pop was her father. Her already dark eyes turned as black as the drain at the bottom of a sink.

And then it was like an Alfred Hitchcock movie, when the room starts spinning around and a person's vision becomes very strange, even though the person is not moving at all. For some reason it's impossible to focus on anything, even if a person tries extremely hard. *Vertigo* is the name of the movie I'm thinking of. Vertigo is the feeling.

When I could finally see, it was clear that everyone was crying, because everybody loved Pop. My brother was actually heaving up and down, and Baby Teeth's face was all crinkled like a wet pillowcase. The words

"Pop died" rushed coldly through me. I don't know how long Lucky was jumping at my legs when I realized he had to go out. After I left the room and found his leash and stood on the lawn with him, what had happened in school started again.

It was as if I wasn't really there. My body was standing next to an apple tree, and my eyes were watching my dog pee, while my mind was wondering if people always died in winter. But really it was as if I'd disappeared. A thousand blue robin's eggs could have dropped from the sky at that moment and I wouldn't have noticed. I had never seen my mother cry.

So why am I feeling this? My mother's not crying now. I look up at the sky. It seems to be fading. How can the sky vanish? I haven't seen her cry since.

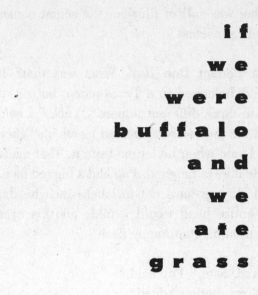

if

we

were

buffalo

and

we

ate

grass

My mother had stopped crying about Pop by the time my father came home that night. In the late afternoon it seemed to me she finally just swallowed her sadness. She walked into the pantry, opened a bottle of scotch, poured a stiff one, no ice, and swallowed.

A stiff one is a double. 'Up' means without ice, and 'over,' full of ice. Pop, my mother's dad, said 'over rocks.' Alcohol was full of illusion; the actual names for drinks were senseless.

Pop drank a Perfect Rob Roy. What was that? It sounded like it belonged in a Texas rodeo, but no, it was made with three different liquors. "Yuck," I said when he told me they were all mixed together. "Yuck yuck yuck," I said when he let me taste it. That made him laugh. He always laughed. Pop had a big red face. He was bald. It was hard not to laugh when he did because his entire head would wrinkle and his eyes almost close from all that happy flesh.

"It's an acquired taste," Pop said.
"Like caviar," my mother added.
"What's that?" I'm a kid, maybe six, maybe eight. I don't know what caviar is.
"Fish eggs." Pop laughed.
"To eat?" I wondered why so many things were not called what they actually were, but by other names: caviar, bouillabaisse. Why didn't someone just say, "We're having some fish stew today"? That's what bouillabaisse was, after all. I'd learned that from Mrs. Connor, Eileen's mother, the last time she had invited me to stay for dinner. I said, "No, thank you"—fish stew?

It was as if words needed to be disguised and so were made into nonsense. But it wasn't the words alone that were dangerous—there's nothing dangerous about fish stew—it was, I decided, what they *could* mean.

"Things are just what they are," said my dad, always so practical. But that wasn't true. A Perfect Rob Roy was not what it sounded like. They all just laughed, which is what Sundays were full of with Pop around. Neither words nor adults made any sense sometimes.

Pop would drive his metallic blue Buick from Brooklyn and pull bags of licorice and bottles of liquor out of his trunk when he arrived. "Make it a stiff one," he'd call to my dad, as if because a week had passed, my father would've forgotten.

"Gotcha," my dad would say, instead of "No kidding, stupid, you have one every Sunday," or something like that. Everybody was nice to Pop. Probably because he was nice first.

We'd sit in the living room. Baby Teeth might be on his lap, waiting for the "Hickory Dickory Dock" rhyme to start, and the Wad and I would sprawl on the couch eating licorice for a while. A roast would be cooking, like always, the air warm with that almost-cooked smell that made my eyes wet.

And Pop would say the same stuff he'd said the week before. "The stock market is worse!" or "That traffic is out of this world." There was always a speech about my mother's delicious roasts and God bless his wife's soul he didn't care that she couldn't cook he had cleaned his plate anyway. "Don't remind me," my mother would say.

And he'd laugh at that, but the sound was low and slow. Sad. Poor Pop. He was all alone. And now he was dead of a heart attack. I knew I'd miss him. I could feel it in the palms of my hands, as if they'd clutched something too hard and suddenly gone numb.

The day Pop died, my father came home, made more drinks, and ordered a pizza. Baby Teeth and I were sent upstairs as soon as we had eaten. We weren't very hungry, so Lucky ate the most, except for the mushrooms, which he hated. Wadstain had left the house earlier when I was out walking Lucky, cursing his way down the driveway, rubbing the tears, like enemies, from his face.

"It's Momma, not Pop, who deserved a massive coronary, don't you think?" my mother said to Dad as Baby Teeth and I climbed the stairs to our room. It didn't really sound like a question, and it was definitely not a joke. Whatever the meaning, my whole body shivered from the chill those words sent into the air. My grandmother had died before we were born.

| | |

Upstairs, I was thinking about what my mother had said. Pop died of a heart attack, so that's what a massive coronary was, I guessed. *Massive coronary* sounded even worse, I decided, than *massive attack*. It was like a war was going on—between life and death? Breathing and not breathing? Some people survived heart attacks, I knew. But who decided?

On her bed, Baby Teeth was reciting something in a singing little voice to the stuffed animals.

"Hey, what are you saying?" I asked.

"Poor little Cleo, he is with us no more, for what he thought was H_2O was H_2SO_4."

"Baby Teeth!"

"What? You could sing with me; we could do like a 'Row row row your boat' . . ."

"That's awful!"

". . . gently down the stream . . . What? Why?"

But I didn't know what to say. "Pop just *died* is why."

"I know. That's why I thought it. Mr. Anzalone told it to me."

Mr. Anzalone, another neighbor, was a chemist. I guess my sister knew as much about death as she did about chemistry. And what did I know? What was I going to say? It's like a war, and then it's over. Sure, say that. Is that any description of life?

"Do you know what it means when someone dies?" I asked softly. She was only five.

"It means they're *dead*." She looked at me like I was the biggest idiot alive. "So Pop is dead now, right?"

"He's dead." I said the words on purpose. If I said them, maybe I would understand something. I waited.

"So when's he coming back?"

I didn't want to answer. I didn't understand anything. I missed Pop, and missing was such a hollow feeling. "He can't come back." My voice was low, like it was coming from the ground.

"Why?" Her voice seemed to come from somewhere else too.

"Because his heart—stopped."

"He won't come back, ever?" She looked at my eyes as if expecting them to say something different from what my mouth said.

"He can't."

"He can't," she repeated. She grabbed one of the animals, a violet gorilla, tossed it to the floor, and stared at it.

"It's true." That moment, unreal or not, was unbearable. Change the subject, my mind said.

"So, Baby Teeth?"

"What?"

"If you want me to stop calling you that, just say so. I'll make everyone stop."

"You started it."

"That's what I mean. If you don't like it . . ."

"I have *another* name, you know."

"Well, I know; that's why I'm saying this."

"No, I like Baby Teeth—it's only *my* name," and she finally smiled, so that her teeth were visible. I loved those small, white rows. Mine had never looked as perfect as that, memory had decided. I couldn't help smiling back, but my sister's satisfaction quickly faded.

Try something else, my mind said. "So, Baby Teeth?"

"So what?" Her dimples always disappeared when she was about to cry.

"Did you hear the one about the cowbird?"

She loved this kind of stuff. Me, too. My dad had told us a lot of facts about nature that he had learned up on his grandparents' Vermont farm, where he spent every summer as a kid. His grandmother, who plowed the fields alongside his grandfather, was a nature lover and a bird watcher.

"Cowbird?" she said, sitting up. "Do they look like cows?" She leaned over and grabbed her gorilla.

"No. They just so happen to lay their eggs in other birds' nests."

"But that's cheating. Cheating!" The dimples were back.

"It's not that bad."

"Yes it is; why isn't it that bad?"

"Because the babies get to have foster parents." I realized I was off to a bad start.

| | |

But she considered this. "Well, that's good. So what about cows and their own nests?"

"The cowbirds never got a chance to make their own nests. Because they used to spend all their time following herds of bison."

"Why'd they follow the bisons?"

"Bison. For food."

"What kind?" She was lying with her head hanging upside down over the edge of the bed.

"What do birds eat?" I asked.

"I don't know—what? What do you mean? Nobody told me anything about bison, so why do you say I heard them?"

"Let's see," I said, "seeds and worms, *bugs* are what birds eat. But wait—slow down. I said 'herd'—a herd is a group—like a *family*, you know, like us, maybe, only if we were buffalo and we ate grass . . ."

"Oh, oh, I don't eat grass!" Her hands went happily into the air, and she sat up. "I'm not a buffalo!"

"So who is? Me?" I blinked, laughing with relief. "Okay, so, the cowbirds eat the insects, get it?"

"But why? Because the bison make them? What kind of insects do bisons make? That's not true."

"Nobody said it was, nutshell. Bison. No. The bugs *live* on the bison. So when they're buzzing around, that's when the birds get them, okay?"

"Oh. I still want to know what kind of insects."

"I don't know—whatever birds like, I guess. So along the way, the cowbirds drop their eggs into other birds' nests, get it?"

"I get it." Baby Teeth finally yawned. "So what about the cows?"

h a
h a

The cows come home eventually. This thought makes me laugh out loud as I reach my driveway. So what if it isn't funny. Stuff that's not necessarily "ha ha" can actually be hilarious.

Why else would somebody, say, Eileen, break into backbends of laughter when the person she's walking

with, namely, me, trips over nothing and falls directly
onto my face?

Or should I say, when she was race-walking ahead of
me just a little while ago, the stupidest-looking activity
this planet has yet borne, I'd mention, if anyone asked
me. My vision got all blurred because I was upset—
because for some unknown reason my best friend turned
into a sarcastic stranger with the heart of a *rock*—and
I couldn't see the lump of leftover blacktop tar at Sagamore so tripped over it, and that's when she decided to turn around long enough to stop laughing and
say, "Hey, you made my day, V, you really did." So
I had no alternative but to, even while my face was
burning raw from blacktop, respond with "Anyone ever
mention you sound like a cow when you laugh like
that?"

And wasn't it hilarious that Eileen decided that *she* was
the one the damage had been done to as the smile left
her face and was replaced with the don't-stab-me-I'll-
stab-you look she had perfected long ago in grammar
school when somebody she didn't like would come along
and try to sit on the empty half of the seesaw Eileen
sat on like it was her property because she was waiting
for me, before she turned right at Sagamore's entrance
and stormed away?

| | |

So I feel a little tilted. Just like my dog. No, that's not funny at all. I stand at the edge of my driveway and look down the darkening road. The streetlights begin to glow beneath their steel black caps. The bus stop is lit across the street. In my mind I see a green VW. I hear it crunch my dog's leg and race away at a hundred miles per hour. I don't see any brake lights. I close my eyes.

Who hit my dog?

Maybe yesterday's over, but that question isn't. I don't like days that end without answers. I'll just keep my eyes open, and we'll see what happens. I look up. One of the streetlights fades, disappearing as quick as it shone, the light sucked out of it. Life can be so hilarious sometimes I don't have time to laugh.

I don't want to think about yesterday. I don't even want to remember it existed. Is today any better? My father goes to the hospital and Eileen is possessed. It's dark out.

Maybe the cows do come home, but I bet nobody ever asks where they've been. I'm supposed to be home before dark. I'd better go inside. I walk up the driveway, another suddenly dangerous blacktop. All I hear are my own black boots trudging numbly over it. Even my feet don't want to go inside.

| | |

I open the back door. Everybody's already at the kitchen table. My mother's carrying a plate piled with hamburgers to the table. "Where've you been?" she says.

"Out." I don't want to look at her. I'm not afraid anymore, I tell myself, not after yesterday. Let her go kill somebody else's dog.

"Just sit down and eat," she says, not exactly slamming the plate on the table. She walks to the sink.

Good, I think. Stick your head down the drain.

"You're late, but it's okay," Baby Teeth says as I sit down.

"How's Lucky?" I say to her. I'm planning on ignoring my mother.

"He's asleep again, and he wouldn't eat any biscuits you left." Baby Teeth is holding a fork loaded with snow peas, her most despised vegetable. Something about the lump the pea makes within the pod disturbs her. I grin as she slides the pile onto my plate with an index finger. She seems to have hit a phase in which everything must have its proper place. Poor kid, she's in for a surprise around here. I hear the water running at the sink. I don't look up.

"Want a burger?" Baby Teeth says.

"Gimme one of those." So Wadbrain's still talkative.

"Is Loretta Getz in any of your classes?"

I look up. My mother is standing with one aqua-slippered foot across the other, her hip leaning against the stove. So we're having a conversation. My mouth is full of snow peas.

I swallow. "English."

"She's not very smart." My mother's in one of her read-between-the-lines moods. Eureka, so am I.

"No, she's not," I say. I drink some water. "She never gets her reports done. Probably because she's been reading the same book since fourth grade. Have you read *Misty of Chincoteague* yet?" I ask Baby Teeth. I smile at my mother, who grabs the newspaper from the counter. I am vicious.

Baby Teeth shakes her head no.

"Good book," I say. "I'll get you a copy if you want."

"That's not what I meant. You know what I mean," my mother says.

Wadnod reaches for another hamburger. "Any cheese around?"

"Can you say 'please'?" Baby Teeth asks him. "Misty who?"

"What are you talking about?" I say.

"She's in the paper." My mother pauses for dramatic effect. Then she says, "Drugs are for idiots."

I can hear my brother swallow. Could that be guilt? I feel my mother looking at me, but I'm busy with my snow peas, a vegetable I like. She's waiting for me to look at her so she can sparkle in motherhood superiority. Where are my sunglasses when I need them?

It's obvious I've got enough trouble already without mistaking quarts of oil for beer because I've been taking what's supposed to be LSD and end up getting my stomach pumped in some awful emergency room like Loretta Getz just did. I'd rather get my name in the paper another way.

Suddenly I see red. What is it?

The ambulance squad had hauled Loretta up the hill from the woods on a stretcher. The window in my English class, a room at the back of the building near the parking lot, was covered with the unbelieving eyes of my entire class.

Black crud dripped from the edges of Loretta's mouth. She had cuts all over her arms. Where was her jacket? She was only wearing a T-shirt and jeans. April is the cruelest month, and it was freezing last week.

The stretcher stopped outside our window as the two EMTs shifted the weight of it between them. And there was Grant Sullivan—a figure from some of my ancient fantasies—walking behind the stretcher as they left. He was carrying Loretta's red baseball jacket.

I I I

That's what's red. My dinner is completely cold. Maybe Lucky will eat it.

Loretta sat up. Her eyes actually rolled, and her mouth opened, though obviously we couldn't hear what she said through the window. But she was close enough so I could see the expression on her face, which clearly looked as if she didn't know where she was. But when I saw it, something like oil replaced what pulsed through my veins. I recognized that look. My mother's face after too many scotches.

I'm numb, everything gone cold on my plate. Isn't alcohol a drug? And isn't it your only friend? Don't say it, my mind says. Don't start a fight. "She's in the paper?" I ask. "So did you see it?" I say to my brother, without question the person my mother should be bothering with this crap. Wadnod just rolls his bloodshot eyes. Maybe he and Loretta would make a good pair. "Read it," my mother says, and drops the paper on the counter. She walks away, the open-toed slippers slapping the floor ridiculously, as if applauding her with each step she takes.

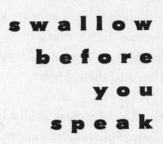

**swallow
before
you
speak**

I wonder if Grant Sullivan is mentioned in the news-paper. I can imagine the line: *A flame-haired rogue, with crooked teeth and a moronic yet disarming smile, was banished to the local emergency room with the oil-laden Ms. Getz.*

A rogue? Banished? Where is *this* coming from? I must have Shakespeare on the brain. 'Courage, man. The hurt cannot be much.' Romeo says that to Mercutio, who has been wounded by Tybalt. Unfortunately, Mercutio ends up dying. Well, okay for Romeo. Let him think what he wants—we all know what's going to happen to him and Juliet. Shakespeare's tragic story is about the 'star-cross'd' pair who love each other but are not allowed to be together because of their feuding families. So they kill themselves.

The guys in my English class really hate *Romeo and Juliet*. Especially Sullivan, it seems, who is always making faces. That mug of his is permanently covered with several thousand freckles, so when he twists it up in literary agony, it looks like he's igniting. Maybe he is.

Some of the females laugh when we read the play out loud, which is what we did today, which is why I'm remembering it. I suppose it's a nervous laughter, and it doesn't surprise me, since some of them've got the attention spans of puppets anyway. I notice a few others swaying around in their seats. They adore the play so much it's like opera—completely overdone. These particular girls I call the Romantics. There are three of that species. They all wear those tinted contact lenses so that the color of their eyes is constantly, and unnaturally, changing.

| | |

Sullivan is big on imitating the Romantics, which is not much of a feat, though he seems to think so. It's only his own ignited mug that's amused when he starts swaying. I can't get that old picture from *Life* magazine out of my mind, the one that shows the results of a 150-mile-per-hour wind galing against a man's face, so that his cheeks are blown out and pinned back to his ears in an inhuman way. Oh, that clown Sullivan. He's always making faces, no matter what's going on. How I could ever have kissed that face, I don't know. Well, it was only once. I guess I had a weak moment last year. It was at someone's party, and it was dark. It was easy to ignore the rest of Sullivan, with the lights off in that basement, and only a few candles burning. I liked his lips okay, but fantasies, maybe, are better left that way.

I don't get nervous, sway, or contort myself in English. I read. *Romeo and Juliet* is full of poetry, which I really like. Except when I'm feeling weak. The love stuff spins behind my eyes like "star-cross'd" secrets. Because I too am full of longing. Well. I'm supposed to read tonight. After I feed my dog the cold hamburger that I'm chopping up right now. After I make sure not to read the newspaper.

The Wadness stands, burps as loudly as he can, and walks away from the table.

"Animal! Did she say anything else about Dad?" I ask
Baby Teeth, who is slowly applying a perfect coat of
ketchup to her second hamburger bun. I watch her from
my seat. She wipes the knife on her napkin when the
ketchup oozes over the edge.

"That we would know tomorrow, is what Mom said."

"Oh." "The hurt cannot be much."

"So, V? Are you mad at Mom or is she mad at you?"

"Both." I get up. "It's okay. Don't ask." Romeo ends
up killing Tybalt for killing Mercutio.

"You can tell me later. And, V?"

"What's that?" 'Stand not amaz'd,' another line.

"Are you scared about Daddy?"

I sit down. "No. There's nothing to be scared of." Of
course she doesn't believe that. She's not stupid. "The
mono test came back negative, right?"

"Right. So?" The perfect bun is now complete. When
Baby Teeth places it carefully on her burger with her
left hand, her right hand seems to automatically drop
her knife to the floor. There's too much anxiety in that
crowded mind.

I bend to pick up the knife. I notice my face still hurts
from my stupid blacktop trip. "So I bet those tests will
be negative too. Law of averages. That makes sense,
don't you think?"

She's chewing a huge bite, but that doesn't stop her
from saying, "I geff fo."

"You guess so. What does Dad always say? Swallow before you speak." I imitate his deep, serious voice. "Remember that now, you little nutshell. If I was somebody else and I didn't know you better, I'd think maybe you needed speech therapy after that one."

Baby Teeth's dimples are pink with delight. "And don't forget he says, 'Don't chew with your mouth open!' " And don't talk with your mouth full. Dad's famous dinner lines. So what if I swallowed the truth. Maybe there's *somebody* around here I can protect. I really am such a good liar. And now, I will take my runaway eyes back to the den.

> . . . *And bring in cloudy night immediately.*
> *Spread thy close curtain, love-performing night,*
> *That runaway eyes may wink, and Romeo*
> *Leap to these arms untalk'd of and unseen.*

Don't talk with your mouth full. Sounds like Juliet's mouth is stuffed with clouds—love clouds. Well, I think I'd rather go back to the chapter in *The Varieties of Religious Experience*. . . .

> *Unsuspectedly from the bottom of every fountain*
> *of pleasure, as the old poet said, something bitter*
> *rises up: a touch of nausea, a falling dead of the*
> *delight, a whiff of melancholy, things that sound*
> *a knell, for fugitive as they may be, they bring a*

feeling of coming from a deeper region and often
have an appalling convincingness. The buzz of
life ceases at their touch as a piano-string stops
sounding when the damper falls upon it.

"Do I hear music?" I say to the air. "Is there a piano-string nearby? Not tonight." Because what I read was: "From the bottom something bitter rises up: a falling of the sound as they bring a feeling from a deeper region as a piano falls upon it." I shut the book.

I feed my dog, my Romeo, my own piano-string, who miraculously eats. Leap to these arms.

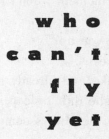

who
can't
fly
yet

Are you awake yet? There's a whispering in the morning air. Everything's okay. Time to get up. There are sleeping dog breaths beside my bed. It's okay. Are you awake yet? I open my eyes.

There's the half moon of the white door, the faded bedroom ceiling. "Nothing loose today." Baby Teeth is awake. She means her bicuspids or incisors or any of her other teeth, which should've started falling out at least two years ago.

But at this moment I don't really care.

"Did I wake you up?"
I close my eyes.
"Mom's awake and already downstairs. If you look in her room, she didn't sleep in her bed. It's weird that Dad's gone; he always comes in and kisses me good-bye."

I groan, which reminds me. My hand dangles over the bed, and the worn green blanket on the floor shifts with stirring dog legs. Without looking I try to reach the favorite spot on his belly where the hair grows the longest. Lucky begins to stretch.
"Time to get up, you know. You're gonna be late. Are you walking or taking the bus today?"

Usually he stretches until his black toes scratch the air and he looks like a flying-upside-down creature. But he can't stretch that way now, not with the cast on. He tried yesterday. The memory slithers coldly across my nerves. Lucky remembers he can't today, right? Please? But the canine earful as he tries to stretch splits the air until it echoes.

l   l   l

"What's going on?" my mother hollers from downstairs as the Plymouth begins to roar outside. Lucky quiets to a whimper, which sends Baby Teeth hurtling across my bed to be near him.

And I am awake. A new day has finally come. I have to go to the bathroom.

It's a good place to be alone. Remember to lock the door. I stumble across the lumpy blue carpet into the shower. There's still hot water; I could weep. Wadstain often depletes the house's entire supply.

Teach the dog to walk. Catch the bus. Find the possessed Eileen. Research this James character. James who? *The Varieties of Religious Experience* is almost one hundred years old—knowing that makes me wonder how many people have read it in all that time. Millions? Ignore Sullivan's face in English. It was definitely his mouth I used to be interested in, not the rest of him. I wanted us to be like matches, ignite on contact. His lips, in spite of *him*, are full, lush, and soft. Damn him, anyway—why'd he have to be such an idiot? Stay awake in math. Go to the hospital. This is my day's itinerary. Where do I begin? No, not in a good mood.

After my shower, I rub the steam from the mirror with the heel of my hand. I see my eyes, dark as ditches in the glass, and wonder who I am, naked and wet. These are my lonely lips.

I dab the cotton swabs above my soft earlobes, brush my lovely teeth, comb my willowy hair, and do a lazy stretch. Towel-dry and slather lotion everywhere. I am soft, I am hard. Subtle gray eyeliner, a dab of blush. Perfume the secret spots. My breasts fill my hands, just for a moment. I turn in the mirror, get a full glimpse. I want to sway with someone on a warm, dark night and feel hands heated with desire everywhere. Then I wrap myself in my robe, wanting to hide, even though I'm alone. My face burns, longing or shame? I keep changing my mind. It's this love/hate relationship I have. With myself.

| | | | | | |

The flat light of April is changing. As it reaches the classroom windows, it no longer glares against the glass, but streams roundly through, sweeping in arcs of richer light, carrying with it the warmth of May.

"The foundation of any romantic attachment is passion." I look away from the windows to the face of Mr. Sanders, my English teacher, as he tells us this. He's sitting on top of his desk. His face, which looks like it was just poured from a blender, all puffy and soft, gets in the way of those words. How is someone supposed to convey anything with a pancake-batter face like that? I

glance around the room. Nobody moves. Not even the
Romantics.

Why are they so still? Oh, I see. It's his choice of
words: romantic attachment. Is love a vacuum? A col-
lision repair shop? Is anybody else thinking what I'm
thinking? Or maybe another kind of attachment is on
their minds, so heavy on the brain, they're cemented
to that word, the beguiling one with three letters, the
s-e-x one, and neither their minds nor their bodies can
forget it. So nobody moves.

If love is a vacuum, does it suck? Oh, stop now! I can't
see what people are thinking; I can barely hear what
the uncooked face of Sanders is saying. It's impossible
for me to concentrate today. Big surprise. But, like
maybe a bird that falls from the nest and can't fly yet
from the ground to the sky, I'm stopped on that word:
passion. And it stays with me all day.

so
pale

Where's Baby Teeth?"

My mother is alone in the car, parked in the school parking lot. Waiting, the thought shudders within, for me.

"Over at that Quinn girl's house. Get in." Both her hands still hold the steering wheel, though the car engine is off. There are shadows beneath her eyes.

I'm standing in the air of the open passenger door, one foot on the curb. I don't want to get in. "Why?" I say. "The tests all came back negative." Something is dragging beneath her words. "Will you get in the car." "Which tests?" I glance around the parking lot—any green VWs? I want to see my dad, so I get in. The air is slack.

"The doctor said he's badly anemic and needs a blood transfusion." The keys clink as her hand switches the car's ignition. "I don't want your sister to see him because he looks really terrible today. I was there all morning, cleaning him up."
Cleaning him up?

We roll soundlessly out of the parking lot. My mother's driving slowly, which is not unusual. I've always thought that she was simply cautious, but I see that she's afraid. It's her hands. They're so pale. Maybe she thinks somebody will run her over.
"Well, what does it mean?" I say and watch her hands gripping the steering wheel. Have they always been so pale? I wonder what she's so afraid of. Baby Teeth said my mother didn't sleep in her bed last night. Did she sleep at all?

I glance away, out the window. All I see are vacant green lawns. The day is bright, but as I look at the sunny sky, it hurts my eyes, as if it doesn't belong where it is. How can the sky be out of place? How can he be so suddenly sick? I see my father in one of his slick business suits, striding across the lawn with his locked briefcase. He's big. He's powerful. He's not sick. How sick is he? "So why is he getting a blood transfusion? Is there something wrong with his blood?"

"Because it's supposed to help. Dr. Sweeney's going to do some other tests, and they've already taken more blood. He's so exhausted he can't even eat. Supposedly, his blood is not acting right." I look at my mother as her lips press sharply closed.

"So the transfusion will give him energy?" The air rolls across my hands as if filled with tiny needles. I look down, see my hands unmoving in my lap, feel they might belong to someone else.

"If it doesn't, they'll put him on intravenous tomorrow; otherwise, he'll get dehydrated."

Dehydrated? Not "acting" right? My hands sting. It's me getting afraid. I don't want to look, don't want to know how pale my hands are. "So when somebody gets a transfusion, they feel better immediately? What about complications? What about AIDS?"

"Oh, Virginia, I don't know. It should work; it's supposed to." A tremor follows her words, so they sound like she doesn't believe this. "And I'm serious, he can't move, so don't be surprised."

Surprised? What could be more surprising than the guy who to my silly kid eyes seemed bigger than trees being unable to move?

"Does he know we're coming?"

"Of course he knows."

I don't ask what I'm thinking. If it were me, I wouldn't want anybody else around. If I were too tired to eat, I'd probably just feel like pulling the covers over my head and sleeping. But if I couldn't move, then what?

Along the approach to the highway, there's a major intersection. "I've been thinking about what I said to you the other night," my mother says, her eyes watching the dangling traffic light.

What night? I do not say this out loud because I do not want to say *anything* out loud to her. And why is she doing this *now*? But okay, it's either last night's charming conversation about Loretta Getz's drug mishap, or it's *Monday's* nightmare . . . my poor Lucky. *I do not* want to talk about it. I glance at my hands, clenched into fists—red, not pale at all.

"Look," I say, hoping to end any chat here, "I don't take drugs."

"That's not what I'm talking about. I'm talking about your dog."

Oh, no, not now. "Is he still in the den?" I ask, because I can't help it. I had moved Lucky's bowls and blanket

there this morning because the den is quiet. I hope he will sleep there when I'm not around.
"He's in the den. I just went home; he's fine. Answer me."

Will this light ever change? My eyes veer away from it, land on the red side of the Dairy Barn. I hate the Dairy Barn because there seems to be one everywhere I go.

Everything is red. I feel like a bull. If it's red, why can't I be in my room, looking at my favorite red box? I have a collection of boxes. I could just sit and peacefully look at the red one for as long as I wanted. I could sing to my dog. It's impossible. I can't ignore her.

| | | | | |

I know my mother never wanted Lucky, but I didn't know why. On Monday, I agreed to work three days a week for Dr. Wheatie, in exchange for Lucky's operation and cast. I said I would start when school ended for the summer.

When Mr. Utley dropped me off, the first thing I did was grab the special green blanket from its place by his food bowl in the kitchen. I fluffed it and smoothed it and laid Lucky down. Then I washed the blood off my hands. With a warm, damp cloth, I wiped all over him, searching for any spots of dried crud the vet might have missed.

I murmured and pleaded in the nonsense language that seems to flow in emergencies and that, really, lies. "It's okay, boy, you're so so good. It's okay, my little dog-head, baby bark." Nothing was okay, but Lucky finally stopped shaking. I carried him, in the new cradle way, to the den, where it was cool and dark, and *I* started shaking. For a few minutes it seemed like I might never stop. Then Eileen called, but I couldn't talk to her; my throat seemed to close when I tried. So I sat there shaking, waiting for Lucky to fall asleep on the couch.

Then my mother called from the engineering firm where she worked. My would-be pet-murderer mother. "So you didn't go to school."

"Eureka," I said. My throat ached.

"Well, how are you?" she asked in her everything's-fine office voice.

Was she joking? Delusional? Pretty good for a person with a dead dog, I thought. I wanted to spit into the phone. She thought Lucky was dead and I would go to school anyway. Such a big heart.

"Poor Lucky; I'm sorry." Her voice strummed with something. Was it satisfaction?

"Lucky's fine too." Saying his name seemed to empty me. I was drained. So how could my eyes fill with tears?

"What?" If satisfaction had strummed, its opposite snapped.

"He's got a cast. He'll have a limp." There was just my empty voice. The tears dried.

"We'll talk about it when I get home."

We didn't pretend with "hello" or "good-bye" anymore, so "What's going on? Who paid for this?" is what she said when she found us later. Lucky was wrapped in the blanket, all peaceful. I was stretched out beside him, reading Shakespeare. Some bright, angry thing climbed into her eyes when she looked at him. My poor dog even tried to wag his tail. Then he howled in pain.

"I am. Leave me alone." I held his tail.

"I'll ignore that. That's a lot of money for a crippled old dog."

"He's not crippled," I said. No, he's not tripping into his grave just yet. She's such a liar. Like I said, she states only the obvious and lies about everything else. "Leave me alone—don't ignore it."

"What did you say?"

"I said, get away from me! Can't you hear me?" I tried not to yell because I didn't want Lucky shaking again. Then another part of me, quiet and calm, said, "Maybe it's you. Maybe you're the crippled old dog."

She reached for me then, and I stood up. Lucky didn't budge, but Shakespeare thudded to the floor. I hadn't

realized I was bigger than she was. "Don't touch me.
You'll be sorry." My hands were fists.
"Well, that figures," she said, as if that made any sense.
But she backed away, and her shoulders slumped and
she looked so small.

My mother began to leave, but then she turned, her
mouth twisted, like a rag being wrung dry. "I never
had a dog. I found an abandoned puppy once, all alone
in a cardboard box on the street, and I brought it home.
It disappeared the next day."

Her voice was filled with something wild. There were
branches in it. Like the ones that smashed against the
living-room picture window in a bad storm, scraping
and scratching. "My sister and I couldn't stop crying,"
she said. "We had meat loaf for dinner that night, and
it tasted bad. We didn't know why; all we knew was
that we had to eat it, every bite of it, before we were
allowed to leave the table. It was dog food—I had
scraped the change together myself and bought the
first can."

My mother's eyes shone like the steel-capped streetlights. The whole room seemed to glow. She crossed
her arms and gripped her own shoulders with those
pale hands.
"I didn't know until later that my mother had drowned
the dog. She told me, no, she confessed to me, when

she was dying. You know why? She wanted me to forgive her."

"Why?" Was that my choking voice? Were those branches in my throat?
And then her eyes were dark. "You tell me, little girl, since you can take care of everything yourself."
I opened my mouth, which made no sound.
"My mother said we were too poor to have a dog. But my father had just bought a new car. So you tell me why, since you've got all the answers."

And then she was big again. So big those words filled the room and the rest of her yanked all sense away with one choking look. I had no answers. The world vanished until I heard the ice cubes clattering into a glass in the pantry. It sounded like someone falling down a flight of stairs. I looked at the place where my mother had been standing. It was just empty space.

ı ı ı ı ı ı ı

I'm numb. The light changes and the car inches forward. "Yes. I thought about it." I sound like a stranger. "Well, I should never have told you that, and I'm sorry I did." My mother returns to silence, her eyes on the road ahead.

Why? Don't say it, my mind says. Not a word. I can barely see her face because she has one of those sleek

haircuts that sweeps forward, in a supposedly carefree
way, around the face. But it looks good on her, like
everything else does, in that tailored, polished way she
has that gives off the warmth of a stone. She's decent-
looking for someone over forty, I decide. The thought
surprises me. Why shouldn't she have told me? Wasn't
it true? It's a bigger surprise when I start to wonder if
I'll ever know her. Does she ever tell the truth? Or is
it me, not being able to tell what the truth is anymore?

where are the windows?

My dad is still green.

All that moves are his eyes. They are unparalleled, really, in their way of seeing everything at once, with a look that digs holes in whatever he's focusing on. In this instance, me.

"Hey, Dad." I stand in the doorway, willing my voice to sound regular, not full of the shock I feel when I see him. A jolt rushes up my legs as if I have jumped from a dangerous height.

"Hey, Virginia." My dad is horizontal under a faded yellow blanket on the steel bed. The blanket does little for his moldy complexion, but the blue of his eyes deepens above it. "You just missed Edward," he says. His voice is as flat as his hair, which is stuck to his head with sweat.

"So there is a God." I roll my eyes heavenward.
At least he can laugh. Then he starts coughing. I want to apologize. He's actually green, like damp moss is stuck to his face. Only his eyes are the same, unwavering blue. "Are you okay?" I say. He sits up slowly, but he *can* move. Relief floods my throat, and at that instant I gulp so much air I choke on it.

"Are *you* all right?" He stops coughing finally and stares at me. Why didn't I just walk in and crash my face into the wall? I'm choking like I swallowed a chain-link fence. That my dad doesn't have on the blue plaid pajamas he was wearing when he left the house yesterday doesn't help. The green-striped pair he's got on shocks me—because maybe they make me feel like he's going to *stay* here. But I eventually swallow and say, "See, Mom said you were . . ."
"She looks worse than I do, don't you think? Where is she? Come in, come in, sit down." He impatiently

waves his hand toward a metal chair with an orange vinyl seat. "And don't tell her that."

I sit. We both ignore the sound the puffy seat makes, and I momentarily feel that the "intestinal" problem of Eileen's father has become my own. "She's getting you some stuff in the cafeteria. You do look a little—drained." My own face is hot. "That's good." He nods. "Drained. Accurate. The way they're taking my blood, I will be drained. She tell you?"
I nod. "Uh-huh." I look around the dismal room. There's another bed, which is empty; another, I'm sure, flatulent chair; and a large shelf near the ceiling with a television set on it that tilts down in an unbalanced way. "Nice place," I say. "Cozy, huh?"

"You said it. Take a cozy disinfectant and call me in the morning. If you're going to die, start in a clean place. That ensures your trip to—what's that place?—heaven." One of his hands presses against his chest. Maybe it's sore from coughing.
"Shut up, Dad. Nobody's going to *die*," I say, which is possibly the most inane statement I've ever uttered. For all I know, the previous tenant of that empty bed just did. I'm in a *hospital*. People croak in hospitals, V.
"Yeah, yeah. I know. Sorry. So, anything happening?" He slides himself back under the covers. The coughing fit brought a ruddy tinge to his face, but it's draining fast.

"Oh, you know. Not much." Right. So tell him some tall
dog tales.

"Yeah. Sure."

My thoughts exactly.

"So how is she?"

"What?" I say. My mind is wandering—no, sprawling.
All I see for a few moments is green, and it's not my
dad's face. It's that damned VW, racing through my
head again.

"Your mother. She looks like hell, as we've already
mentioned. So how is she otherwise?"

"I guess she probably feels like hell too," I say. I can
feel myself blink. This room is too small.

My dad rubs his hand over his eyes, winces, looks at
me. "It wasn't always like this," he says. "She used to
be . . . like a light switch. You wouldn't believe how
much she used to laugh. The reason I married her is
because of the way she used to slap her leg when she
laughed—as if that might help her stop, because she
couldn't once she got going." He slaps the air with his
hand. "You wouldn't believe it. . . ."

Embarrassed, I feel my forehead furl. I'm uncomfortable because I do—and I don't—want to hear this.
What happened? I really want to know, but it's too
much to ask that now. "She's not laughing too much
these days" is all I say.

"We do the best we can, isn't that right?" He's still wincing.

The black telephone has been pulled so close to his bed, its cord looks ready to snap from the wall. It sits on a high, wheeled table, next to a box of tissues and a maroon plastic pitcher.

"So you've been working?" I say.

"Nah, just in case they need me." We both gaze at the phone. "Deadline, you know."

My dad's in advertising. A long time ago, he was one of the first to put live animals in TV ads. Sounds dumb, but his company made a fortune. Now he does "concept" stuff, which really means all he does is talk.

"Big account?" Why am I saying this? Go ahead, tell him the smell of the room is making you dizzy.

"Nah, small potatoes. Toothpaste. Some print ads."

He can move. He's not exhausted. I wonder if he's faking.

"You could watch TV." Oh, I see. My brain won't stop chattering these stupid things because it's not used to my dad like this. So green and helpless in that huge bed. It makes me nervous.

"Not today. Got a headache. So tell me something."

"What?" Why is his hair plastered down on his head so that he looks like somebody in a cartoon? Does he know it? So that's what she meant by "cleaning him up."

"Anything. How's the lucky dog? Today's favorite philosophy flavor." His hands rest on the blanket. I don't know why they look so big.

"Wrong kid," I say. "I'm not Baby Teeth."
If it's possible, his eyes frown.
"Okay. Lucky ate breakfast, he walked a little, hooray. What I learned in school today is the foundation of any romantic attachment is passion."
He doesn't blink. "What the hell does that mean?"
"You tell me."
My dad groans. "*Attachment* is the wrong word there. Try *engagement, entanglement,* even better. Now you're talking. That's English, the class?"
I nod, impressed. He understands.
"No—*attachment* didn't sound very philosophical. *Adumbrate, mundification—those* are philosophical words. So what are you reading?"
"Shakespeare." Adam who?
"Good luck."

His green face is turning gray. Is it the day's diminishing light? A nurse squeaks in on white, rubber-heeled shoes. There must be two hundred pounds inside that tight white uniform. We all say hello. She checks his pulse with one hand and, with a free pudgy thumb, starts a stopwatch.
"Am I still here?" he says to her. "Still ticking, or is it the watch?"
She smiles without showing any teeth. "Still here.

Dinner will be up in an hour, then your transfusion."
And with that, she squeaks out.

"Then your dessert. Is that what she said?" He sighs.
"That is one *big* nurse."
"Less is not always more," I offer.
"More what?" My mother walks in, carrying a carton
stuffed with food. Looks like she robbed the place.
Well, my dad is skinny enough to eat it all.
"Just what the doctor ordered," my dad says, closes his
eyes, and is asleep.

ı ı ı ı ı ı

Am I really awake? I'm home, in bed. My eyes are
open. I want to reach up with my hand and grab the
darkness, hurl it out of the way. Where is the soothing
moon? It is so dark tonight I can't even see my hand
in the air. But my eyes don't care. They stare against
the dark, wanting to see. See what? I can't take it.

On my elbow I lean and switch the tiny lamp on the
wall above my bed into brightness. The beam hits my
pillow, but I can see figures beyond the direct light.
There's Baby Teeth sleeping, her eyes closed. The sight
tugs at my throat, like I might cry. I look quickly away
and see Lucky on the floor, his front paws dreaming in
rhythmic twitches. I'm quiet. I don't wake either one
as I rise. Then I find myself downstairs, as if I have

just woken up. As if upstairs, I saw nothing, because nothing was there, and I didn't exist. It's unreal.

There's a blue glow in the living room. It's the light from the den television spilling in. My naked heels make no sound as they cross the glowing carpet. I stand in the doorway. There's a blur of motion on the television but no volume. An empty glass sits on the wood table next to my mother's chair. Legs tucked beneath her, knees poking whitely out from her robe, her head in her hands. "Can can can," she moans. Can what? What can? She doesn't see me.

Can't? I must have breathed in a big way because she lifts her head.
"V." Is that an echo?
"Mom?" She never calls me V.
We look at each other. Where are the windows? The walls? I see nothing but the daze of her eyes.
"I dunno wha'sgonna happen," she says, the words reckless as her unfocused eyes.
"I know that. I know, I know." My words tumble. They are rocks, because I am made of stone.
"Can'happen, can't," she says.
"Stop, okay," I say, "please stop, it's okay." There are those emergency words again, landsliding out in their lying way. It's not okay.

| | |

I'm beside her chair. Though the glass is empty, I can smell booze. It burns, both sweet and sizzling, in the air.

"Why don't you go to bed now," I say, but in a voice that stabs the air.

My mother looks up at me, and her head sways. She's out there on the high seas and I'm dizzy. She's that carved figure on an old ship's bow, drenched in the whipping sea spray. I wonder if she can really see me.

"You need to go to bed." My voice is drenched. I sound older.

"Doeddn' matta'."

"Let's go. I'll help you." I reach for her as she stumbles out of the chair. She's actually listening to me. As she lurches, I catch her arms. She can't even walk.

"Doeddn' matta'."

But it does. As we weave up the stairs, she sways heavily from my grip and pitches against the wall. I step behind, one stair lower, and push from the back. What else can I do? My eyes fill, but it is only colors. Green. Ice blue. The aqua robe. I push. She feels so small.

She is small as I lean her against the prized mahogany dresser in her bedroom and her hands skid across the top, knocking the perfume bottles into a clunking heap.

She thuds down the side of it before I can reach her. I flick the light on, and her face lies on the gleaming surface. She drools on the polished top. I yank the bedcovers down, because it's either hurry or leave her kneeling on the floor and I'm desperate to end this awful scene because there's a howling in my lungs that has taken my breath away. So hurry, drag her to the bed and let her fall into the soft sheets so she can stop hurting herself, please no blood, though she won't know she's hurt until she wakes up, until she's not drunk anymore. And then she can pretend it never happened, even though there's a black eye fresh on her face to show it did, it really did.

It does matter as her swaying head sinks into the pillow and her robe is twisted like a big rope around her. I try to loosen it as a gurgle rises from her throat in a baby-sounding way, and she closes her eyes, since they are heavier than anchors, and the ripping sounds of her breathing finally wind down into hushed grabs of air, and eventually drop into smooth breaths that sound like she's finally part of the world as I stand there.

Yes, it does matter. My mother is a wreck. As I look down on her sleeping face, her mouth open like Baby Teeth's when she is dreaming, she seems impossibly younger than my eight-year-old sister. As I swallow whatever rises in my throat, the unreality of the night heaves through me. This scared little child-mother of mine, no matter how much I hate her, needs me. It's either her innocence that lingers like a clump of cement in my throat as I try to swallow or the disappearance of my own.

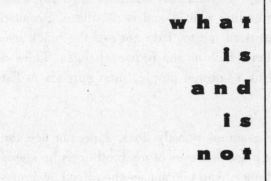

w h a t

i s

a n d

i s

n o t

Sometimes the night never ends; it just breaks into light and we pretend. I am alive, though I tend to forget that when I'm pretending, and I'm fifteen. I have sweeping dark hair and hazel eyes that turn green when I cry. Sometimes I rub my hands together, maybe just to see if it's really me. I wear the glasses I'm supposed to wear when I'm in the mood and whenever I remember my sunglasses because the day hurts my eyes. Maybe the pretending has torn the edges of who I am, so the result is a frayed and sensitive me.

If the night never ends, who can see? The day boils down to pretending what is and is not there. Because she does not want me to, I do not see the black eye on my mother's face as the bruise changes, fades a blotchy red to a tattered purple, then spreads to flat green.

Because he assumes nobody does, I do not see the increasingly bloodshot eyes of my brother as he stares past me at dinner. And I do not see the raised eyebrows on Baby Teeth's face that settle more frequently into surprise as she watches and helplessly learns this pretending game. I wish I could tell her she doesn't have to play, though if she's to survive life in this house, she will.

So I do not notice that on the days that we do not go to the hospital, she spends every afternoon at other people's houses now. And I especially do not see the absence of my father at dawn when he does not kiss the sleeping Baby Teeth good-bye before he climbs down the stairs in his solid brown shoes and goes to work. And I do not see his absence as I pass his empty chair at night when I walk into the kitchen to feed my dog. The last thing I do not see is my tilting, limping

Lucky as he waits by his empty bowl, or the image of the vile green VW that hit him.

So what do I see? That I have learned to pretend so well, I can do it with my eyes open. April has ended, and its cruelty too, I hope, when we weren't looking, or were busy pretending, or maybe while we slept.

So it's May. And what does it bring? April showers bring May flowers. Well, really. I try to remember, uncertainly, if there was a lot of rain last month. No. But please flower anyway, all over me. I'll keep my eyes open. Maybe it won't happen all at once, the way change seems to. Now that's something. Change blooms.

I I I I I I I

Here at school, everything is the same. Standing by the wall of windows across from the science rooms, watching people fill the hall since the bell just rang, I'm safe. Math is over for one more day.

The brick school building was designed into what are called wings, and each subject has its own. One side of each wing is lined with classrooms, and the other, with windows. Science is located in C wing, down the hall from the administrative offices. Even my feet feel safe as I stand on the worn stone floor. They are warm and pleasing in my shoes. What's wrong is this bad taste in my mouth. I don't know what it is.

I cross the hall and glance through the tiny window of the classroom door to see what's taking Eileen so long. People are grabbing their books and rising from the lab tables; somebody's pushing the door open. I spot Eileen in the back. Oh, no, Parker paired her with Grant Sullivan for lab. Their Bunsen burner is still burning on the scratched gray table. Sullivan is talking to her, but her back is turned toward me, so I can only imagine the pained expression on her face. Sullivan laughs, amusing himself again, I suppose. Poor Eileen. I lean in, about to call out her name and save her, but I hear her laughing as she bends to pick up her books. When she straightens up, there's something on her head. Is that a hat? Did I miss something? Connor has placed an ugly black hat on her head.

I cross the hall again. Change can bloom, but it can also wilt. What's with the hat? Just seeing it makes me feel like something is really *wrong*, like, what's Eileen trying to cover up? Maybe it's me, unfathomably paranoid, but maybe I don't want to make peace with Eileen at this moment after all.

We've been avoiding each other for days now, ever since Sagamore. I'm not blaming her, no, not completely. But put a lid on it, I think to myself, that feeling of being willing to apologize to Eileen even though the fault wasn't mine. Just to end the stupid fight. Because where is my friend? I need her. We've had a million stupid fights. But I suddenly remember how nasty she was at Sagamore. Who does she think she is beneath that dumb hat? Some mysterious movie star? No, not now. I don't want to interrupt Eileen's performance. The bad taste in my mouth is worse. So I turn. And then I see her.

With this impossibly long hair, so long it falls past her hips. Like a black horse's tail, it sways across her black jeans as she walks through the hall, passing me. I wonder if she sees me as she walks by. She doesn't seem to, but she passes me so closely it's as if she moves through me, so close I can smell the leather from her jacket. What kind of boots is she wearing that make no sound? I have no choice but to breathe her black motorcycle jacket in as she glides by, surrounded by the darkness of her clothes, this oh-so-cool and silent-footed girl, who I have never seen before.

I wonder where she came from. I wonder if she's real. Because as this stranger walks by, the bad taste in my mouth disappears. My mouthful of unanswered questions vanishes. There's never been anything like this woozy, wonderful breath. Let the wind in.

| | |

I notice a book sticking out of her back pocket. She walks by so close I can't help but read the title on the ripped paperback cover: *Rimbaud*. As I wonder who that is, it doesn't even cross my mind to question why the world so suddenly seems to be neither frayed nor sensitive, in place.

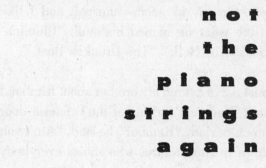

not the piano strings again

In the tree's clear branches
Fades the sound of a hunting horn,
But lively songs still skim
Among the bushes and sky.
Let the blood laugh in our veins,
See the vines tangling themselves.
The sky has an angel's face.

Let our blood laugh in our veins. Not bad. That's Rimbaud. How do I know? When in doubt, go to the library. Arthur Rimbaud, born in 1854, was French. He was, primarily, a poet who also wrote "prose poems" that he called stories. Already he seems unusual, and I like that. I also like what he named his stuff: "Illuminations," "A Season in Hell," "The Drunken Boat."

I made the mistake of asking my brother about Rimbaud when I spotted Wadstain lurking at the cafeteria door during my lunch period. "Rambo?" he said. "Ain't you seen that clown in the pictures who shoots everybody on sight?" I laughed then and I'm trying not to now as I sit at the kitchen table, remembering. The truth is, I like my brother, even though he is a stoned and mindless creature.

It's late afternoon. I'm trying to get my homework done, including some doomed algebra problems, but my mind, once again, is wandering. That stupid Eileen hat makes an appearance. I fled the scene outside science, not so sure that I'm interested in knowing the face beneath the black fedora. Nobody wears hats, and even though I like unusual stuff, I don't like it on top of Eileen's head. I mean, really.

Lucky is at my heels. He hobbled under the table himself, like some arthritic old beast, which he is *not*. Even though he looks like he might tip over when he shuffles around, he can walk. So Slow Motion is his middle name. Lucky's getting better.

My dad's getting worse. The blood transfusion was like a Band-Aid. It didn't fix anything, though after the nurses removed the drip twelve solid hours later, my dad walked out of his room and sauntered up to the nurses' station to say that he was checking out. It was a big joke at the time, supposedly, like the hospital was a hotel, but the next several days were less than funny because he couldn't even sit up, much less say anything.

Instead, he began to sleep nonstop. They had to wake him up for meals. He even slept through the changing bloom of my mother's black eye. Actually, she covered it with makeup when she went to see him. Yesterday was the first time in days he was fully conscious, and yesterday is also when he started to gag and twist all over his bed.

As I look out the kitchen window, my brain has a mind of its own. It tosses the reminder of yesterday into my head and starts this roaring behind my ears. Oh, the questions. Not that I even need to ask them. Who hit my dog? What's wrong with my dad?

The phone rings. It's Baby Teeth.
"Have you ever seen a red spider?" she says.

"Not lately. Where are you?"

"I just came out of the Connors' bathroom. He's in there now, crawling up and down. What should I do?"

"Who's in there?"

"The spider, on the wall, V."

I worry about my sister. Especially about her being worried. "Why do you have to do anything?" I say. At least it's Eileen's house, someone I know.

"It goes up and down on this invisible thread, up and down."

"So you've been watching it. Does it look unhappy or wounded?"

"I'm watching it, uh-huh. No, it's okay."

"Good. So why don't you leave it alone? You should get back here soon, anyway. Lucky needs you to sing to him—he misses you, I can tell. Is Eileen home?"

"No. That's a good idea; I don't have to do anything— I miss him too." There's a big silence. Did she hang up?

"Hello?" I say.

"Hello. Are we starting over?"

"Baby Teeth."

"What? Is Mom home?"

"No. So where's Eileen?" That hat surfaces in my brain again.

"I don't know. Should I mention this?"

"Mention what?"

"The spider. Eileen's mom made me a ham sandwich.
So you don't know how Dad is."

"No, clamshell, I don't. But don't say anything, okay?
Maybe that spider's just moving in, setting up its web
in there. I guess it likes the wallpaper in their bathroom.
Which bathroom is it? The blue one downstairs?"

"Downstairs, yup. It's so red. Do you think he's okay?"

"Red is a good shade to be, so . . . so vibrant." I look
out the window. The grass does not move, but something
sad happens in the air. "Yeah, I bet Dad's okay. He's
been sleeping a lot and maybe the sleep will help him.
So promise me you'll leave that spider alone."

"I will. What's vibrant?"

"Alive, nutshell. Do you want me to come get you?" I
might cry. I am such a good liar.

"No, I'm coming."

"What about the spider?"

"I already promised. Then what will happen? After the
web, I mean?"

"Well, maybe, Baby Teeth, that's the talking spider
we've all been waiting for—maybe when you go back
to visit she'll introduce herself."

"Oh, sure, V. I have to go if I'm coming home."

"Hurry up," I say, but it's the dial tone I'm talking to.
"Don't be scared." Maybe the spider can hear me. Or
maybe I'm talking to myself.

I I I

There was a book I read once, about this huge guy who used to kill little animals by accident—because he didn't know how strong he was and he would love them to death. What was that book? *Of Mice and Men*. But Baby Teeth is not incredibly strong—is she?

I look out the window again. The grass still does not move. There's nothing sad out there. The algebra problems loom before me. I hate algebra. It's all about calculation, which has nothing to do with real life. I open the James book instead. Oh, no, not the piano-strings again.

> . . . *The buzz of life ceases at their touch as a piano-string stops sounding when the damper falls upon it.*
>
> *Of course the music can commence again;— and again and again—at intervals. But with this the healthy-minded consciousness is left with an irremediable sense of precariousness. It is a bell with a crack; it draws its breath on sufferance and by accident.*

Well, he can say *that* again. It's amazing to me that when I open a book, there is always a miracle somewhere on its pages. An entire novel can be miraculous, but if not, a paragraph here and there, sometimes a single line, maybe even just the *voice* in the book is enough to slay me. To send me off, to relieve me of my self and whatever predicament I happen to find myself in at the time. "Draws its breath on sufferance and by accident," indeed. Sufferance is my father and the accident is my dog.

But if the next paragraph mentions anything about bone marrow, I believe I might just drop dead. Forget that the grass doesn't move; neither will I. This morning was my father's bone marrow test.

I was there yesterday, wincing in the background, when my dad started twisting all over the bed. It was like he was suddenly plugged into some horrible socket. His blanket slid to the floor in a fast and hideous yellow heap.

"But what is it? What is it?" my mother jumped up from her chair and yelled, loud enough to reach him if he were in some other hospital, in another town, even.

My dad's left arm was connected to the intravenous saline drip by a fingernail-thin plastic tube so transparent the fluid was visible. What color was that tube? Like old spit, and it ended up attached to the flesh of my dad's forearm with a needle battened down with a piece of thick white tape.

My dad must've forgotten he was connected, because in one jerking heave he twisted his entire weight over to his right side, and the needle flew out of his arm. It swung through the air and his arm started spouting blood like that's what it was meant to do, like it was some kind of bloody fountain. My mother's mouth dropped open and my eyes shut tight without my knowing. When I opened them, my mother was leaning over the bed trying to reach the button on the other side that sends an electronic signal to the nurse station—a panic button, just not with the word *panic* written on its blue surface. While her pale hand pushed, I saw my mother's face strain as if she were trying to lift a thousand pounds.

That's when I stopped breathing and my father started gagging, but there was nothing for him to upchuck because the only food he had been able to keep down was this saline solution and only because it was attached to him, in vivo, that's what that means, through the veins and to prevent dehydration. So he was twisting and gagging and coughing and moaning and bleeding all over the place and the bloody sight of my father's arm only exaggerated the white look on my mother's face. My dad was saying, "What? What? What?" And then he suddenly stopped moving, and I gasped for air because I had forgotten how to breathe and suddenly the blanket was in my hands. And then my mind said tourniquet, but that's when a nurse swished in above her raspy stockings and wrapped his arm with gauze and a towel that she grabbed from the drawer of the night table and stopped the spewing blood as quickly as she might have turned off a faucet. She checked his pulse and pressed his forehead with her hand.

And nothing moved until the nurse swished out of the room. Was it all a dream? No, blood was everywhere. An aide came in with towels and a mop, swabbing at the mess. After a while Dr. Sweeney appeared in the doorway and said hello to everyone. We all looked at him. He cleared his throat and announced, yes, it was an announcement, that "It's possible a bone marrow test is called for. We've run out of possibilities."

"Possibilities?" The word came in a white-hot hiss from my mother's throat.

"Listen, Doc," my dad said, coughing, "quit with the possibilities. Do you know what just happened to me?"

"That's why I'm here, Mr. Dunn. I'm sorry. I wish I knew . . ."

"Just find out what the hell is going on. What was that? Some kind of fit? Was that a convulsion? You want to do a bone marrow test—do it. Every part of me feels like it's on fire, including my goddamn bones."

That's when the flesh on Dr. Sweeney's forehead began to shine.

This place is a tangle of vines. Rimbaud was right. The buzz of life ceases. . . . There are no pictures of him in the few books I found. I wonder what kind of mouth he had. Was it lush and soft, would I want to kiss him? If he was alive today, maybe we could run away together. In reality, I'm looking out the kitchen window, leaning my echoing head on my arm, and what I see is like a bell with a crack. I don't see any angels in the sky.

h u s h - h u s h

Do the Watusi. There is a word, far from any dance, for what this house feels like. My breath is like wind on my arm, the place is so terribly still. Even with my siblings home, each of us in separate rooms. Wound tight as the metal spring behind the clockface, or deliberate as the ticking hands beneath the glass, we are waiting. Somewhere in the ticking, even Lucky wandered away.

Waiting for the mother to return from the hospital. For news about the father. For the wind to disappear. My sister's teeth to show. My brother's eyes to clear. Eileen Connor's hat to burn. Ha ha! Romeo to Juliet! The silent-footed stranger, the Rimbaud, to appear again, maybe. The wind will disappear, I am certain. I am, too, such a good liar, but this we know.

If only my mind could catch up to my thoughts. My thoughts have a mind of their own, and pass through, uninvited, like this is my party and I'll do the Watusi when I want to. But all I can really see, as I sit at this table in this kitchen on a May afternoon, all I'm certain of, is Baby Teeth's cellophane-covered sandwich.

Baby Teeth placed it on the table with such care when she came home a little while ago, it began to look as though it *meant* something, that somehow it was important. What can a ham sandwich mean? All dressed up with nowhere to go. That's not it, no. Like an offering, yes. A sacrifice, maybe, to the gods. What gods?

The kitchen door swings open. My mother doesn't have to say a word. I see her eyes. Black as the bottom of the old empty well in Elaine's backyard. She steps over the threshold, pushes the door shut behind her.

"I'll get everybody," I say, grabbing my books from the

table. As I cross the room, I hear the chair legs drag across the floor, the slump of my mother to the creaking seat.

As we enter, Baby Teeth dashes to the table, slides the wrapped sandwich to my mother's elbow. "See what I got, Mom? You could have it." She places her hand on my mother's arm. But my mother doesn't move. One hand over her eyes, the other spins the lazy Susan, which makes a hushing sound. The salt and pepper, the sugar and spoons, go around in circles. We've eaten almost every meal of our lives at that table.

My brother and I glance at each other and walk to the table. Do we want to protect Baby Teeth? Or is that innocent hand on my mother's arm what I can't sustain, what hurts my eyes as I see it? Edward sits on a chair, his legs seesawing beneath the table. Can I hear his teeth clench? I can hear. I grip a chairback, my feet on the floor, watch the spinning. Hush-hush, the sound comes from the turning, hush-hush. The cellophane shrieks under the busy fingers of Baby Teeth's free hand. Even the air is loud, but none of us says a word. Why would we? We know about Dad.

Edward grabs a napkin and starts tearing it to bits. Usually he rolls little paper balls, which he tosses into his mouth, but he doesn't do that now. "So I guess you got some news," he finally says.

My mother looks up, her eyes heavy-lidded. "Your father . . ." And she sees Baby Teeth, stretches her arms around my sister. The spinning slows.

What? I can't hear. My mind says no. Oh, Baby Teeth, don't cry. A somersault in my throat. "What is it?" Words actually surface, because I have to say something, because Edward is groaning, because the salt and pepper have stopped spinning and I see only my mother's eyes. It feels like I might tumble into them, instantly sink to the dark bottom. Cover Baby Teeth's ears, but I have to know.

My brother is almost doubled over, his chin inches from the tabletop. Napkin pieces are scattered. Can't you sit up? I want to scream and kick his chair. But my mother doesn't move, won't say what it is.
"So it's a blood thing, Ma? Like leukemia or somethin'?" says Edward.
"The damn blood," my mother says.

The air sounds like static, like some invisible hand is searching for a radio station. Or it's raining on the windowsill.
"No such thing as blood cancer, right? Not cancer," Edward says.
"Not cancer," Baby Teeth says. Does she know what cancer is? Her eyebrows are raised, surprised. Tears fill her eyes.

| | |

"No, no." There are the pale hands, around Baby Teeth. "Cancer would be good news." A sneer crosses my mother's face. "If it was, they might at least be able to treat it. Radiation, chemo, whatever. No. Not this time." She closes her eyes. Her eyelids as pale as her hands. "Twenty cases across the country in twenty goddamn years. That's what Dr. Sweeney said, why it took so long to find out."

Is she talking to us? I might fall down. I have no legs. I could learn, maybe, that trick in which the tablecloth is yanked from the table but all the plates, piled high with steaming food, stay in place. What am I thinking? Where's Baby Teeth? I can't focus. My seeing blurs.

"What about Daddy?" Oh, there's Baby Teeth's little voice, but it splinters the still air, like the heels of some great big beast. *What about Daddy?* I want to scream. But no, no. I can see my mother's shaking hands, my brother's twisted mouth. The dimples have fled my sister's damp face. Hush-hush. Daddy, she said, the word kicking through the air, knocking the wind out of the way. Is that my sister's hand in mine? Hush-hush. My mind is spinning. The air is splitting. The sacrifice has already been made.

"Daddy's not going to make it."

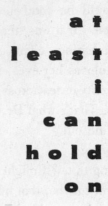

at least i can hold on

It feels like somebody else's life has inhabited my body. How is that possible? It's not. I said it *feels* that way. My mind is spinning. Why don't I go crash my head into a wall so everything will stop, so I can catch my breath. What breath?

At my worst, I am shaped like a piece of wood, and as if hurled into a thrashing brown river, I am waterlogged.

Each step I take seems to be submerged. No. Knock knock. Who's there? Any sanity home? Stop. At best, there's a lock on the bathroom door. I can rest my aching head on the lumpy blue carpet—everything in this house is blue—and spin around in peace. I can slip my hand between my legs, slide to the dark, hidden place, where it's warm. I'm safe there; I'm not afraid. At least I can hold on.

But it's like somebody else's life. Having a sick father is like having a secret, only in reverse. Even if somebody, namely me, wanted to talk about it, nobody, namely Eileen, would understand. Why does my water-logged self without sanity say this? I called Eileen after we all stumbled out of the kitchen the other night. I said, "My dad is really sick. He's not going to get better." And she said, "Oh." She didn't even attempt to say, "Oh, what a terrible thing!" No, nothing like that. A simple "Oh" was enough. Did she say "Oh" when she meant "*Oh!*"? I said, "Sorry about Sagamore. You know I was only kidding." But she didn't say anything. Maybe it's that ridiculous hat of hers, blocking her ear passages. Maybe it doesn't matter. Ever since I heard "Oh," like "Oh, it's raining," I don't feel like talking to anybody anyway.

But that "oh" didn't stop Eileen from telling everybody else. By the time I got to school the next day, I swear I was famous. The way people looked at me, eyes all snapped open like jack-in-the-boxes, maybe I had grown another head. Maybe my skull was expanding at an enormous rate so it became twice its normal size and was about to burst. God help all the bursting heads of the world. God who?

It's a certain kind of fame, though, to suddenly be so different from everybody else that they can't tear their toy-box eyes away.

So why doesn't some clown hand me a microphone and call a school assembly so I can stand onstage to make an announcement. *Yes*, my dad is dying. He has contracted a rare blood disease called acute milofibrosis, which destroys his red and white blood cells. Since the cells are—toss in a little oxygen, please—what the blood actually consists of, without those cells, *Ta da!* That's it, folks. Curtains.

With all those eyes veering sideways, as if they're not really looking at me, I feel like I'm being followed. I'm being spied on. But it's somebody else's life.

I find myself in my stupid red gym uniform with some rubber ball between my hands and wonder how I got there, or I'm up in room 524 North at the hospital and suddenly all I see are my father's blue feet as they slip from the covers because they always do these days. They were never blue before, or maybe they were. But at home he always wore the tan suede slippers I gave him for his birthday a couple of years ago.

Maybe I'm in the backyard, moving in slow motion with my dog. And the same old questions begin to spin through my head, erasing time, erasing me. Who hit my dog? And then I want to ask, what's wrong with my dad? But that one's been answered, even though I guess I don't really believe the answer is true. It's so unreal, it's surreal. Even if he is turning blue. Where am I? I can't even answer that. I don't know where I am. Time is spinning. I am spinning. Yesterday was hell. Is today any better?

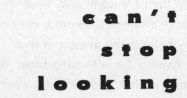

**can't
stop
looking**

Yesterday was hell. Or was it the day before? We piled into my dad's hospital room like potatoes stuffed into a sack. The air was so stifling, I thought my eyelids might dissolve, which would be tragic. Because then I would have to see *everything*. It was bad enough that we discovered the windows in the hospital room were built so that they will not open. Ever. Germs, I suppose.

My mother had gone to the cafeteria. Edward's ponytail swayed as he strained at the stubborn metal window frame before we realized we were doomed to the same suffocating air forever. When I leaned over to get a better look, I noticed his hair was tied back with more hair. So he had snipped off a clump of his own and twisted it up around like rope. Oh, that brother of mine, what a character. But as I watched him from the edge of my awful vinyl seat, something kicked behind my eyes.

My hand pulsed with a desire to reach up and touch that well-conditioned ponytail. What was happening to me? I actually gasped and looked at my hand—who did it belong to? Like I said, somebody else's life in my body. The sound I made filled the room, it was so quiet in there.

Heavy sleep breathing had been the loudest sound in that room for days, except for the moments my dad would murmur stuff we couldn't understand. But it was a relief to hear him mumbling, even if it was incomprehensible. The sounds convinced everyone, especially my mother, that he wasn't in a coma. We whispered when we were in the room. Our whispers became normal, which, when the thought crossed my mind, was not at all normal. There was Dr. Sweeney, and then came a urologist, a neurologist, and packs of medical students, at different times of day. My mother would tell them all to keep their voices down.

| | |

"It won't budge," Edward said, hushed and low.

"Oh, well," I answered, in the good-news tone of the true imbecile, as if what was in front of me wasn't bad news. I could even feel an imbecilic grin on my face, the kind that spreads like a stain and has to be wiped away with a hand to get the face back to normal. A grin that landed tears in my eyes for no reason.

"You said it." When I looked at him, he was grinning too.

It felt like we were kids again, but not in that way we used to have of wanting to kill each other, way back before Baby Teeth was born. Not in that way of convincing the other to play hide-and-seek in the basement and promising not to leave as we turned the lights off to play, and then one would very intentionally walk out of the house. That was so long ago. We had actually liked each other then, and making each other cry just seemed to be a way of expressing it.

As I grinned at my brother standing by the window, I wondered whether childhood had hurt us, or did life just start to turn people into strangers? I guess I stopped smiling because my brother's face turned brooding and serious. He came over to my chair, laid his hand on my shoulder. I might have broken into tears. Was he bigger and stronger than me? I wished he was. As I looked up, I saw there was something different about him. His eyes were not bloodshot. They were unbelievably clear.

Then somebody laughed, and I turned around. Baby Teeth. She was seated on another vinyl monster behind me, her fingers sprawled in her mouth, searching out any wobbling incisors. She looked as if she were eating her hand, and Edward laughed. Baby Teeth removed her hand, wiped it ceremoniously across her sleeve, and said, "Like rocks."

My mother returned with a steaming cup of coffee and sat on the room's only upholstered chair, which Edward had dragged in from the lounge one day. It was flecked with brown and gray dots and had plastic arms and legs, but at least she could sink into it. "Did you see the doctor?" my brother asked.

She nodded. "The head of hematology is interested in your father's case, of course. He wants to try some experimental drugs. Keep your voice down."

"What did you say?"

"That we can discuss it after we know what the side effects might be. Shhhh." She blew on the steaming coffee, which created a small tide in the cup.

We all looked back at my sleeping dad, the way people look at Christmas trees, I bet. Can't *stop* looking.

While he slept, Baby Teeth dozed in my mother's lap. I swear that sweltering room would put anybody to sleep. My mother opened a magazine, though I didn't notice her turning any pages. My brother just stared out the window a lot. He took his pocket watch apart and put it back together several times. That watch had belonged to Pop, my mother's dad, before he died. It was silver and opened and shut with the most satisfying *click*. There was a flying eagle etched on its cover.

I sat back in my chair by the end of the bed, watching my dad's feet move while he dreamed. Eventually they would slip from beneath the yellow blanket and I would drape a piece of the white sheet over them, so when he woke up, at least his feet wouldn't be cold. Would he like his slippers? They were still at home.

I began to wonder what it would be like if he never woke up, and my hand froze with that thought. I was numb and I was sweating. I wanted him to wake up immediately. Then I wanted him to wake up when I wasn't around so he wouldn't have the chance to ask me questions, something he always did.

"What are you reading?" he'd say. He'd be looking through me with those eyes of his and I'd mumble something dumb, sounding like an idiot, probably, because at this point it felt berserk to imagine having a regular conversation with somebody who'd been twisting all over the bed and turning green. Somebody who couldn't keep any food down. Somebody who looked like a shrunken version of my father and whose hands were suddenly the biggest, strongest part of him. So what was I going to do?

I'd manage to say, "I'm sorry you're feeling so bad," or something like that, because then an inch of a smile would widen his mouth, which had begun to look unnaturally pasty, as if it could not smile if it wanted to, and some life would spring into his eyes.

What was I going to do? I found myself staring at his hands, and I guess I began to feel guilty because I didn't want him to wake up and start asking me questions, because I suddenly felt weightless, like I was made of air and might float away. I decided I'd better get out of the room for a while. My mind said flee. My heart said stay. When the conflicting voices became a rubber band ready to snap behind my eyes, I sprang out of my chair.

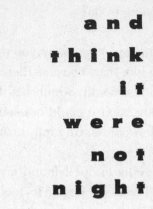

**and
think
it
were
not
night**

Maybe I could fly. There were five flights to the hospital cafeteria. It didn't occur to me to wonder how many steps in a flight, because as I left my dad's room and stormed down the hall, I kept my eyes on the black-and-white spotted floor. I ignored the open doors to other rooms, where other swollen, moaning patients lay. I ignored the elevator, where there might be a freshly croaked body on a rolling table.

| | |

I had never known glee until I saw the red EXIT sign
and swung open the thick fire door beneath it. A cool
gust of air hit me in the face, and that's what I wanted,
to take my mind off those awful voices inside of me.
They were so loud, I heard nothing else as I hurried
down the steps. Not even my own footfalls. I saw my
boots beneath me, stepping without a sound. And then
the picture in my mind changed, from my black boots
to the ones of the silent-footed girl. Her name is Jane.

I stepped into homeroom the other day—when, last
week?—and there she was, standing in the back of
the room, the tattered maps of the world on the wall
behind her. Her smile bloomed before that tired
scene.

After Ms. Labianca, the homeroom teacher, called the
roll, she asked Jane to introduce herself. And this Jane,
like some Mediterranean model with a deep olive complexion that glowed, sauntered up the aisle, sauntered
in her silent black boots and skintight faded jeans with
her motorcycle jacket draped off one shoulder. Nobody
moved as she walked, but she didn't seem to notice.
At least, not in a way that made her uncomfortable.
That smile just bloomed.

I thought of a scene I'd just read in *Romeo and
Juliet*.

The brightness of her cheek would shame those stars
As daylight doth a lamp; her eyes in heaven
Would through the airy region stream so bright
That birds would sing and think it were not night.

Then the stream-so-bright Jane just turned on her heels
and said, "Hi, guys, I'm Jane. Nice to meet you," and
smiled that smile.

There's usually a period of time, anywhere from a couple of days to a few weeks to forever, that nobody talks
to the new kid, depending on what kind of case someone
is. But not with Jane. Everyone started talking to her.
Somebody was always swooping around her. Crowds,
in fact. The boys were in love with her, their eyes lit
up like Shakespeare's lamps. Except for Sullivan, of
course. Too busy with Loretta Getz.

Sullivan, in my opinion, is with Loretta for two possible
reasons: Her brain is still so saturated with oil, she
cannot respond normally and flee from him. Or she is
as mentally unformed as he is, and they belong together
happily ever after.

Even the Romantics talked to Jane. It was easy to see
jealousy there. All someone had to notice was the way
they kept jerking their heads around, flapping at themselves like chickens when they talked to her. Jane made

them extremely uncomfortable. Maybe it was the jacket. Or her incredible green eyes.

So everyone but me was already talking to her. I wasn't talking to anybody. But it was particularly awkward changing into my ugly gym suit next to her. It's not an easy task to be half naked next to someone who is not only a total stranger, but who happens to be gorgeous as well. When I dared look at her, and I tried not to, she seemed to already be looking at me, smiling in that blooming way that started a fire on my face, I was so embarrassed.

What was she smiling at? What did she think? Were my tits too big or too small? I had a pretty good body, but not like hers. Hers was perfect. My shoulders were too big, my hips narrow. I was shaped like a telephone pole. When our eyes caught, it was as if magnets pushed against each other—that strange field in which one veers away from the other. I'd end up staring off into the distance, suddenly looking through mindless space.

The moment finally came—when?—the end of last week, when we spoke. We were sitting in the back of French class. Jane and I had, coincidentally—or does anything happen by accident?—arrived early. There were only a few people around. I wanted to ask her about Rimbaud, this mysterious character who wrote stuff like

Over the roads, by winter nights,
without a home, without bread, a voice
would clutch my frozen heart: "Weakness
or strength: you exist, it's strength—
You never know where you go or why: go
everywhere, answer everyone . . ."

But I couldn't ask. It was as if I'd forgotten how to talk.
Rimbaud seemed so brave. I wondered if Jane was too.

Then a couple of Romantics passed by and said to me,
"Hi, Le Chien."
That's when Jane turned her smile on me. "Why do
they call you that?"
"I'll tell you later," I said.
And these are the first words we spoke.

Later that day I was standing in front of my gym locker,
supposedly changing. Really what I was doing was staring at the lock because I couldn't remember the combination. Did I exist? Jane showed up and was watching
me.
"You haven't told me why they call you Le Chien."
"Oh. It's from a poem." Answer everyone, Rimbaud
wrote.
"You were a dog in a poem?"
"No," I said. But I was not in any frame of mind to tell
any stories. I had just heard that my father was going

to die. My father was going to die, and I had to go to
school like he wasn't. And so I suddenly couldn't remember things like my lock combination, or how to
talk sometimes. Then I looked over at Jane. Her face
had gone pale. What did she care about me? I thought.
"I'm sorry," I said. My voice swayed. "I'm wiped out."

"I can tell." She nodded in an easy way, bending toward
her locker. Her impossibly long hair swept across my
arm then, soft as wind.
I was ready to bust. There were no words I could think
of. "It's just, my dad, well, it's . . ."
"Your dad." Even her voice was soft. She was kind.
"You know?"
"Everyone does. Sorry," she said, looking directly at
me. She didn't pretend I wasn't there, like everyone
else—or if I was, that I had two heads.

"Me too. Everyone's acting like I've got a disease."
"Do you want to talk about it?"
"It's just unbelievable. One day he's fine—and now he
can't even swallow a pill." I felt my face burn, but I
didn't care.
"What're the numbers?"
"What?" I said.
"Your locker."
"Twenty-two, three, seventeen."
She opened my locker. "Change," she said, "or you'll
be late."

"So what."

"So Greene will give you detention."

"So?"

"So then we won't be able to walk home after school."

Miraculously, I could think of nothing to say. At least one person in the world would speak to me.

maybe
i'm
not
ready

Sometimes I wake up in the morning and I don't know why. My eyes just open. I mean, there I am. If I don't move when my eyes open, it's easy to feel like I don't have a body at all. Like it's only what's in my head that exists. If I don't move, it's my brain that feels the sensations my body would normally experience. My mind feels the blanket covering me. It's warm in my mind, and peaceful. Not to have a body at all. I wonder

if this is what it feels like to be dead. I wish my dad
would wake up.

I open my eyes. Baby Teeth is staring at me.

"Do you ever sleep?" I say.

"I'm an early-riser individual, different from you," she
says.

"I'm awake," I say. "Isn't that enough?" I yawn and
listen for the usual stirring. Lucky yawns beside my
bed. My dog warms me; my mind can feel it. I am
alive.

"So the phone rang really early," Baby Teeth says. I
look at her nightgown, its frilly, short sleeves, its roses
spreading over the white cotton. She's holding a vanity
mirror before her face as she sits on her unmade bed.
With two fingers she tugs her mouth wide, peering
inside for any sudden changes.

"Maybe you'll be a dentist when you grow up," I say as
I blink the sleep away and lean on an elbow. My other
hand reaches down to greet the dog. His wet nose
nudges my hand.

"That's not what I think. You know when you go to sleep
and you have hopes?" Her dimples deepen.

I only nod. I would wait forever for an answer to that.

"Don't be funny when I tell you, okay? Maybe I'll have
real teeth when I grow up."

She's serious, poor kid. "Of course you'll have real

teeth. Since you waited so long for them, they'll be drop-dead gorgeous, I bet."

"You know I hope so. Don't you want to know who was on the phone?" She slides the mirror under her pillow.

"More than anything."

"It was the hospital."

"That's not funny." I sit up.

"No, really, it was." Baby Teeth stands. "Daddy's awake!" Her hands rise above her in victory, then she jumps on top of me. "Really awake! Sitting-up-and-eating awake!"

I can't even breathe, but I don't care. My arms grab the roses as the thrill rushes through me, and I hold on.

| | | | | | |

I usually walk to school, but since today is already a special event—he's really awake!—I decide to take the bus. I'll see my dad later, of course. He'll be sitting —he'll make sense when he talks. I'm going to meet Edward and Baby Teeth at home, after school. Baby Teeth has chorus today, so she'll be late.

It's really spring. The air's still dewy, but there's a crisp edge to it as I cross the lawn on the way to the bus stop. The grass is a lush, deep, unmowed green. Nothing will ruin this day. Even the bus is on time.

I climb the two steps, and the first thing I see is the cloud of Eileen's hair in the back of the bus. Oh, delight. But wait, no hat. It's a positive sign—maybe things can be the same. I decide to sit next to her, bump my way down the aisle, and even smile as I approach. My best friend's eyes jump wide as they see me, then shoot to the window. Oh, please.

I sink into the thick black seat. "How's it going?" I say in a regular voice. I decide to ignore that she's been ignoring me. How long has it been? Two weeks almost.

"Pretty good." Her hands grab the pile of books from her lap, and she holds them in front of her, some kind of barricade.

She's wearing a bracelet I've never seen, silver with turquoise stones.

"Nice piece," I say. I lean over and drop my books to the floor. I step on them so they stay in place.

"Yeah, thanks." She laughs like I don't know her.

What's your problem, I want to say. When did your new life that doesn't include me actually start? Maybe she's waiting to see if I'm mad at her. She must know what an idiot she was for telling everyone about my dad. Well, I won't let it ruin this day. My dad's awake. Change the subject, my mind says. What can I say? Well, every sophomore in school is reading it. Go ahead. "So what do you think of *Romeo and Juliet*?" I say.

"No big surprise—it's too sad for words."

So are you, my mind says. Guess I'm still mad.

Eileen is looking out the window as she speaks. "And it's not easy to read, with all those wherefores and what fors; I have to stop at every line and try to figure out what they're saying."

"What's so sad about it?" I ask, trying to be nice as I speak to the side of her head.

"You're kidding. Aside from the fact that Romeo gets banished and Juliet is tossing down poison and all these other people are getting *killed* . . . they both *die*."

So she can actually say the croak word. I'm impressed. "They die? I guess your class is further along than we are." I play dumb. I just want her to look at me, something she hasn't done since I sat down.

"Everybody knows the story, Virginia. It's famous, so I guess you're just being an idiot." She looks at her watch, not at me.

"We're only up to Romeo getting banished, in Sanders' class." I still play innocent, though I'd like to kill her for that. When did she get so mean? Do people just wake up vicious one day? It's like *I'm* the one being banished.

"Oh."

There it is again. *Oh.* Okay, my friend, we can both play. In the story, Romeo is only trying to stop a fight between a band of Montagues and Capulets, and a Montague is murdered. Romeo gets attacked by the murderer, who *he* murders—that's why he gets banished

"Yeah. So their *death* is the sad part?" Maybe if I just rub it in, the tears will leave my eyes. Maybe *I'll* feel better.
But Eileen doesn't get it; she just looks at her watch again. "It was so drawn out and fatiguing, what could be worse?"
Your hat, I think, that stupid, filthy, dust-covered rag. I am stone.

The bus jolts to a stop. Kids pile on. Oh, great, there's Sullivan. Eileen seems to sway next to me. Have I been missing something here? The Romantics are the swaying types. Don't even think it. Is there something going on between Eileen and Grant? I glance at her, but she has turned to the window again, so I get a good view of the back of her head.

Sullivan ignores us and takes a seat several rows in front. I watch the back of his head, waiting, I guess, for some kind of sign. Sullivan and I never speak to each other anyway. It's an unspoken rule. Well, I don't know about this day anymore. Let the wind in,

I think—maybe as it blows past, I'll realize this moment will too. Baby Teeth knows what she's talking about.

ı ı ı ı ı ı ı

I'm disturbed. Now there's an understatement. No, really. I feel like I'm floating. Ever since I got off the bus. It's not anxiety. It's some whatever trying to surface inside me, and I just can't grasp it. It's like attempting to climb the gym rope, but my hands keep slipping. It's not even a feeling; it's deeper than that. It's something I *know*. Except, only a part of me knows it, not all of me, so it doesn't connect to the rest of my thoughts yet.

I'm sitting in math trying to concentrate. I'm watching Mr. Giamano's big math head as he scribbles algebra problems on the blackboard. I'm trying to concentrate, but it's hopeless. Algebra is nonsense. There is no emotional meaning to math at all. It occurs to me that I would never say this aloud, even though I think it.

That's it. I wonder when I stopped saying what I thought. I'm suddenly aware that I seem to have stopped talking. I mean, I didn't say what I *really* thought on the bus this morning with Eileen. That I was hurt and angry and why was she avoiding me, and by the way, only fools wear hats. I know we used to talk; all we did was talk. Now I feel I'm getting somewhere. I'm climbing to the knowing. What is it?

I must be staring because I hear my name. "Virginia." It's Giamano.

"Yes?"

"Have you finished the problems?"

"No," I say, looking at the yellow scrawl on the blackboard. "I haven't even started." Then I smile at Giamano's dark math eyes, because I have actually just learned something.

He looks at me blankly. He must think I'm the one who isn't making any sense. But I am. It was the day of the hit-and-run, back there when life was cruel, in April, when I stopped talking.

| | | | | | |

I'm standing in front of school watching everyone stampede toward the buses, deciding whether I will walk home or not. I have time before Edward and Baby Teeth get there. Jane appears by the door. "Want to walk?" she says.

"Sure," I say. I'll *try* again to be myself, the one I was before all these questions started hounding me, I think.

"Let's go the back way. It's nicer."

"So did you grow up here?" she says as we walk past the redbrick side of D wing.

"You could call it that." Stop it, I think. Be straight. "I

was born two towns away. We moved here when I was three." That's better.

"I'll show you the woods. Have you been there yet?" I ask. We are behind the school now. I look into the English class windows because I can't look at Jane. I don't know why. Stop asking.

"Uh-uh, not yet. This girl, Loretta somebody, was telling me about it in the bathroom the other day. You go?" Jane is subtle. I'm impressed. "Not really . . ." Just say what you *mean*, V. "Only on my way to somewhere else—I don't hang out there."

Jane nods in that easy way. "One look at Loretta was enough to keep *me* out of there."

We laugh.

We reach the dirt path and start down the hill. The trees are green and full again; the air is fresh. It really is spring—there is nothing cruel in the air. I love the way the dust tumbles when my feet hit the ground.

"Do you like sports?" Jane is behind me.

"Some." That's true. The only thing I hate is gymnastics.

"I've noticed you're pretty good," she calls.

"Years of slavery, you know?" Am I good? At the bottom of the hill I stop. "How about you?"

"I want to faint when I see a field hockey stick," she says.

| | |

The smile doesn't leave my face. "I like your jacket."
"Oh, thanks. But I see you have *natural* ability, good coordination. It's obvious in basketball, anyway."
"Well, I don't know." That's true too. My face starts to burn. Why? Because she's been watching me?
"Yeah, it's great down here. It smells *so* good." The leather of her jacket crunches in the nicest way as she spreads her arms open. "I just want to take it all home with me, you know?"

I look around the clearing at the bottom of the hill. There are some branches on a few dogwoods that still hold their pale buds, but otherwise the open flowers rise from the branches like small clouds. "Me too. We can sit down for a while, if you want. You can tell me, I don't know, what you think of the neighborhood, or whatever," I say.

She looks like she belongs in the woods, like some kind of olive animal. The green of her eyes matches the leaves of the maple trees.
"I can tell you one thing." She looks directly at me with those eyes as she wraps her arms around a big old maple. Anxiety replaces my breath. What is wrong with me? Maybe I'm not ready. "Please," I say. What do I mean? "I think about you all the time."

In addition to my face, the rest of me is now surrounded by flames. Why does this girl make me feel like this?

I can't believe words can actually come out of my mouth at this moment, but I manage to tell the stream-so-bright Jane I'll take her to the pond, one of my favorite spots.

It's strange to think Shakespeare must've meant her when he wrote that line, since he's been dead for about four hundred years, but that's what passes through my mind. Something is happening to me. At least I'll cool off at the pond.

**bigger
than
both
my
hands**

My father's flesh is the color of fire trucks, but the flames must be coming from inside his body, because he is out of his mind. As we walk into room 524N, my dad is bolt upright on the bed. His pajama shirt is nowhere in sight, and his back is as stiff as a ladder. It looks like the blankets and sheets, scattered in twisted clumps on the floor, have been thrown from the bed. The air in the room is like electricity and sends a charge surging down my spine, so I feel I'm plugged in through my feet.

Before his head has even turned to us, he's talking. We might be across the street, his voice is so loud. Like a siren. Can his voice be on fire too?
"So glad you could make it. Everyone yes, and the snow is deep. It's almost time but I didn't tell. Yes, yes, the curtain is up, my grandmother is there, the baseballs and everyone. It's here, but not with the shoes, sit down. And you . . ." And how his voice changes as he points to me and my siblings in the doorway, like his chest is full of mud . . . "you, you . . ."—his big red hand is pointing and he's yelling, "Go to Schwab's. Go to *Schwab's.*"

My mother, who has been standing before the sink in the corner of the room, whirls when she hears him. "Daniel, Daniel!" She's at the bed. "It's the kids. Daniel, stop!" and reaches for his face with her hands.

The water is still running in the big stainless steel sink. "Help me," she calls to us. "Hand me washcloths—make them cold." I hear her kiss my father. Only then can I move. I see my brother's mouth hanging open and I grab Baby Teeth's hand and we are at the sink. Did we walk? There is a buzzing in my ears. I can't tell if it comes from inside me or somewhere else. As if I'm watching myself, I lean over the sink and grab some damp white washcloths lying in a heap, and let the cold water soak them.

Baby Teeth is at my side, her hands hanging on to the back pocket of my jeans. And my brother is there. Without a word, we become an assembly line as I hand each chilled cloth to Baby Teeth, who hands it to Edward, who gives it to my mother, who presses some piece of my father's bony red chest with it.

"Where are they?" my brother says. "Where are the nurses?"

And my mother doesn't even turn around as she answers, "A bad drug they gave him. It's a fever—it'll break. Hurry."

"When my grandmother comes, everyone must rise," my father says. He's all curled up on the bed. I glance over, but I'm too afraid to even look at his face. My dad's head is cradled in my mother's arms. I look back at the rushing water.

Nobody says anything. The air smells like it's on fire. The cold water soon freezes my hands so bad I can't feel the washcloths anymore. My fingers are red and numb and I begin to drop the wet cloths before they get to Baby Teeth's hands. I can't keep a grip, and fury and frustration surface, like mist blurring my eyes. A puddle starts on the floor and my feet begin slipping. Baby Teeth slips. Edward tosses the blanket into the puddle and at least we don't fall down. My father starts to sigh. "I'm so tired, just so tired all the time." It's his regular voice.

"I know, honey. Don't worry, I know," my mother says.

"What's this?" he asks, and we all turn from our places to look at him, but in his eyes is something I've never seen. Those aren't my father's eyes. They're so red, it looks like they're full of blood. "Who's here?" he calls, like he's some kid lost somewhere, and the lonely sound of it fills my throat with a swelling lump. What does he see?

My mother is patting his hair, caressing his gaunt face, and he falls forward with a choking, stuttering groan that becomes so light and simple it finally stops. Nobody moves.

A nurse appears in the doorway. From the corner of the room I can see that she's frowning. She tugs at the collar of a peach-colored sweater that she wears over her uniform and walks briskly to the empty side of the bed, where my mother is not standing. "Let's get him back to bed now, all right?" she says. She and my mother grip him by each scrawny bicep, and he leans back like maybe there's not a bone in his shrunken body. The nurse is careful not to knock the tube in his arm.

"I'm taking your temperature now," the nurse calls to my dad, even though she's beside him. He's staring at the ceiling, and she slips a thermometer into his mouth.

The thermometer is attached by an elastic cord to a plastic box fixed to the belt at her waist. My dad's chest is heaving, and he spits into the air.

The burning fire of the air is smoldering now. As if through a cloud, I see the pink flesh of my dad's chest and neck, the blue in the pulsing veins, and the most pale skin on the underside of his arms, so that his flesh looks transparent. Almost like the wax paper we used to press on top of leaves in art class. Tape smudges and purple bruises from the syringes cover his forearms. His arms open and rise into the air, palms up, and he reminds me of somebody else. It's the Cadillac driver, Mr. Utley—the way his arms went up at the vet's— like he was surrendering.

"It's a hundred and three," the nurse says as she removes the thermometer from my dad's crumpled lips and glances from the blue plastic square to my mother. "That's better than it was an hour ago. The doctor's making rounds—he'll be here soon." Her voice is gentle, her eyes soft.
My mother nods. She's breathing hard, as if she has been running, and the nurse looks at us. "Great job, everyone."
Baby Teeth sputters.

The nurse quietly finds my dad's pajama shirt in a heap of sheets at the bottom of the bed and hands it to my mother. "The antidote should make a difference soon," she says. My mother holds the shirt as the nurse fiddles with the IV beside the bed, nods to us, and asks, "Do you want me to help with the bed?"

My mother shakes her head. "I'll do it, thank you." Her words sound pushed out, forced off a gangplank.

Before the nurse leaves, she says, "I'm sorry no one came sooner. It's difficult when the shift changes."

My brother is standing beside my mother, and Baby Teeth has not moved. Her hand is in her mouth. "What anecdote?" my brother says. My hands find Baby Teeth's shoulders and we walk over, close to the foot of the bed.

My dad's eyes are closed now. He opens them. "Hey," he says when he sees us. Those are his eyes, but they're still red. "Hi, guys."

"Daddy!" Baby Teeth calls, and springs to his side.

"Have I been asleep all day, huh?" He looks at my mother. Her face is drained. She tries to smile, her hands fumbling with the bed sheets. Edward finds another blanket in the closet. This one is green.

"Getting chilly again, oohh . . . where's my pillow?" he says, and looks blankly around him.

My mother says, "We're just straightening up." And they manage to get his pajama top back on. It's the blue plaid, the same one he left the house in. When was that? A long time ago.

ı ı ı ı ı ı

When they are scared, box turtles tuck their heads between their upper and lower shells, then bend the shell closed over the remaining gap. But someone observing them wouldn't know they were scared. The turtles simply appear shut, as if they never had any legs or heads to start with. Considering that hiding is the only defense they have, their performance is a good trick.

When I was ten years old, I found a box turtle by the fence in our backyard. I used to climb the fence, stomping the wide white plank at the top so my banging heels echoed in the woods. I would feel so powerful, so connected to the world. When I picked the turtle up that day, its legs jutted out and grabbed at the air. I was surprised at how strong it was. It actually pulled me forward, and I almost dropped it. The shell was bigger than both my hands. I was running before I knew it and didn't stop until the turtle lay inside an empty cage in the basement. Before boxes, I collected cages.

After an hour, all the turtle had done was stay closed. I knocked on its speckled, mud-colored back, but it wouldn't answer. I turned it upside down, and since its feet were also pulled in, the million wrinkles covering its legs were gone. I tried to pry the shell open with my hands, but it wouldn't budge.

I left it alone and went upstairs. I found Lucky in the yard and played the I'll-throw-the-stick-where-did-it-go-it's-in-your-mouth game because he loved it. When I returned, the turtle had flipped over onto its back, and something inside me dropped. Earlier, I had run my hand over the turtle's orange belly and felt how soft it was. Upside down would be a dangerous position if the turtle was outside in the wild. So was it surrendering?

I offered it lettuce and nuts. The nuts were no good—they were from a can. But the turtle still wouldn't emerge. I brought it back, finally, to the place I had found it. I pretended to be a tree and stood very still next to it. I wanted to witness the initial poke of its head out into freedom. It didn't budge. I felt like an idiot and left.

After dinner, I went outside again with Lucky, and the turtle was gone. It wouldn't move while I was there, but it somehow knew when I was gone. It wanted nothing to do with me. Turtles are cold-blooded reptiles.

| | |

I mention turtles because of their shells. The events of the past several weeks have left pieces of me scattered everywhere. What I need is something to escape into. A protective shell. At least this day is over.

At the hospital, once my dad had his pajama top on, my mother told us that the fever and the fire-engine rash he was suffering were part of an allergic reaction to one of the drugs the hematologist had prescribed. At least it helped wake him up, we lamely joked. And even though my father could see it on his own skin, he didn't really seem to believe what was happening. He said he was fine. We didn't mention the Schwab's thing.

In the parking lot before we went home, my mother told us that Schwab's was a famous drugstore in L.A. where people went to be "discovered." People who wanted to be movie stars. Well, none of us did. As far as I knew. My father had been delirious. As my mother buttoned his pajama shirt when the delirium was over, my dad said, "No more. I'm not the blood works guinea pig."

"What do you mean? You won't try any of the new drugs?" my mother asked. "The head of hematology wants to discuss it with you."

"We can talk about it at home," my dad said.

| | |

I lie in bed, watching a curve of the fading moon through the curtain. I think of turtles because they are so slow. My dad told me back then it was a box turtle—he didn't even have to see it when I described it. It takes turtles forever to get anywhere, though it seems in an instant they are gone. Dying is like this, I've decided. My dad's coming home tomorrow.

when
the
world
comes
back

It's morning. I'm waiting for the keys of heaven. Maybe some Bleeding Hearts or Little Miss Muffets will bloom soon. Bunches of Forget-Me-Nots are up already, I see. Those are the scattered mounds of blue sometimes planted around trees because they flower best that way, with a little shade in sight. Forget-Me-Not.

| | |

Such elaborate names for these lopsided stems that arise in the dirt, and such special care. I see people pruning and watering. But not everybody likes a forever pink dwarf hydrangea. I'll say. Me, for one. Not my style, those pink ones that go limp so easily. A little hard rain and kerplunk. Well. How do I even know the names for flowers? Why am I even thinking this stuff? Because my dad told me.

I'm on the bus. I look out the window. The world and its cut lawns, its careful plantings. Eileen is nowhere to be seen, which is unusual. Is she sick or something? She's always on the bus. But I'm actually so relieved when I discover her absence that I stumble over Loretta Getz's purple-sneakered feet as I make my way down the aisle. I just don't see them. Am I color-blind? Or are they even there as I pass? Maybe she means to trip me. I wonder why there is such mystery in the air now, and when, especially, it will stop.

But there's Eileen in homeroom, and eureka, she's ignoring me again. That stupid hat again. That foul rag, symbol of all unspoken. It turns away from my voice when I say, "Hey." I stare at the back of it for a moment, wondering how fast it might ignite if a match accidentally landed on it. Well, I've had it. I say, "Nothing's up, is it, Eileen? I'm just not really standing here, am I?" When I turn away, there's Jane, handing me a note.

| | |

After the bell, Eileen stops me in the hall. She doesn't look sick; she looks mad. Can lips quake? Hers are. We're standing in A wing. Social studies. How appropriate, since my long-lost friend seems to have become a social reject.

"What's with you?" she says.

"You've got that backward, don't you think?" I say. You're the one acting like an ax murderer.

"Cute. How come you haven't called me?" Her hat quivers too.

"Maybe this is just a bad dream," I say. "Last time I did, you had no comment, remember? No, wait—that's not true. When I told you my father was really sick, you said, 'Oh,' like, 'Oh, have a nice day,' remember?"

"Don't put words in my mouth, Virginia. Just because your father's sick doesn't mean he's going to die, you know, I mean, he's too *young*, anyone can see that, for one thing."

And I finally understand. She simply can't believe it —she's too afraid. Oh . . .

My head is full of rocks. "But he *is* going to die, don't you get it?" Every word is a rock. I think I just might sink into the ground from their weight. "He's all sprawled out on this hospital bed, and you should see my mother—she looks like there're black pits dug under her eyes. . . ."

Her face twists. "So he really is."

"There's nothing else they can do. He's coming home to-day." The rocks are in my mouth. He's coming home to die, my mind says. Maybe I'm already sunk.

In an instant, both her arms are around me, her breath in my ear: "I can't believe it's true, V, it just can't be." But it is. No sooner has she hugged me than she disappears; the warmth of her breath goes cold in my ear. It's true, I want to shout. But she's gone. Until this moment some part of me has been rock hard with disbelief; yet now that I've actually said it out loud, all of me can hear it. I might throw up. My hands are sweating. The back of my neck is soaked. He is going to die. Maybe I finally believe it. Because I feel like I'm choking, like my mouth is full of dirt.

When the world comes back into focus, it's the wall I'm staring at. What wall? Here in A wing. I hear a voice, glaring as the sun in my eyes.

"How's your dog?" It's Sullivan's voice.

"Are you talking to me?"

"Well, yeah." He glances around the empty hall. "We're the only ones here." He shrugs and laughs.

I look at his eyes, which are open wide, like whatever it is that's on his mind is too big for them. My eyes are wet. I don't trust him. "What do you care? How do you know about my dog?"

Sullivan shifts from one foot to the other, as if his

shoes are the wrong size. "I'm just asking. . . . It's a small town, you know, that's all."

My eyes are wet. His are on fire.
"So what's it to you?" I say, blinking, all traces of anything soft, like fog, away. I feel my fingers trembling. I can smell something in the air. I know that smell. What is it?
And then his smile fades. "Dunn, I thought you were a clever babe, but something is preventing you from *seeing*. Where was your *pal* when your dog got hit?" As Sullivan walks away, his feet don't leave the floor. He slides, as if his shoes are too big.

The late bell rings. What? Where was Eileen? But that lingering smell, what is it? The burnt stuff at the bottom of a cup. That's how I connect it. Danger. I can taste it.

This is nuts. I shake my head to clear it of Sullivan, which is not hard—dumb coward hasn't talked to me in a year. I'm late. I have to get to class. I have to get to my locker and get my books. My hands shake so bad I hide them in my pockets even though nobody else is in the hall. As I reach in, my fingers close around the note Jane has given me. I don't have time to read it, but I read it anyway:

Hey, V! Listen to this one—

*   'Do I care anymore about the world's noises
and the study hall's sounds? What will I do with
the others around me . . . each head, weighted
with sleep, hangs over the desk before it . . . My
head leans into my hand, listens to my heart
beat with Thimothina.'*

*   Brought to you by the great R. It's not a
poem—it's a letter Rimbaud wrote—but a fake
one. Fiction in letter form, get it? Guess he had
study hall too. And that's about what it's like
last period as I wait to walk home with you.
Are we walking home today? You are my
Thimothina. J.*

I walk into social studies. It's the wrong class. I have
English first. All of me is shook up now. That feeling
of somebody else's life in my body. And who is this
Thimothina?

at
the
path

Everybody leaves me alone. I make it through English and math unscathed. The only snag I hit is in my elective, Western philosophy.

"So, Virginia," the teacher, Mr. Burr, says, "which chapter from *The Varieties of Religious Experience* did you choose?"

" 'The Sick Soul,' " I say.

| | |

People, of course, laugh. I guess the title would be funny—if it *was*, that is. But we're in philosophy, so it's not. People can be so stupid sometimes; I wonder if they'll ever change. Mr. Burr, since he's smart enough to have read the entire book, ignores them.

"So if I were to ask whether you believed in God, based on your experience with that particular chapter, what would you tell us?"

"Seems to me it's more about what's inside people than about God." I'm not in the mood for God.

The chapter was full of discussions about different people struggling to make decisions about what they believed in—dust-to-ashes kind of stuff, like destiny and religion. That's where the piano-strings were.

"I see." Mr. Burr nods his head. "That's a chapter with an interesting story about Tolstoy in it, for those of you who don't know. In which Tolstoy forgets 'how to live,' or, if you like, finds that life has no meaning." Mr. Burr looks at me.

"It is," I say. "Life lost all meaning until he was transformed spiritually—until he heard the piano-strings again, I think."

"And do you disagree with his experience?"

"I don't think it's possible to *disagree* with somebody else's experience. I mean, if that's somebody's experience, how can someone else say it isn't? That's illogical, so it's not the question."

"That's true." Mr. Burr nods again.

And the moment miraculously unsnags, because he doesn't ask me what the question *is*. What a relief, since I don't have an answer. Instead, he starts talking about Tolstoy.

| | | | | | | |

In French class, Jane asks me to walk again, and I almost say no. I want to get home early because my dad will be there today. But that doesn't make any sense, really, because we're going to pick him up later, anyway. And I *want* to go with Jane, so what's wrong with me? It seems like I'm scared. Of what?

"Can you walk today?" she says. "We can go to the pond again."

I stand by her desk on my way down the aisle. "I'm not sure," I answer. "But you can; you remember the way."

"Not without you," she says.

There's a new lump in my throat.

"It's so soothing at the pond, like a massage for the senses, you know? I need it, and so do *you*," she says.

Soothing is a good word for it. I think I smile, though

I feel I might start choking; I can't imagine saying a word. But I don't have to speak, because she keeps talking. I like that about her. Even though people are walking by and making noise, Jane doesn't care. It's her world. She's so comfortable in it. And then there's me, thinking that Loretta Getz's purple sneakers are trying to trip me for no reason.

"If I wanted to be idiotic about it, I'd even decide the pond was serendipitous," she says.
"You don't feel like being idiotic?" I manage to say. What else would I say? Does she really mean she doesn't want to go without me?
"Not if I'm the only one," Jane says.
"I guess it's hard to find serendipity on your own." Serendipity is the gift of finding desirable things by accident.
Jane smiles like she knows exactly what I mean, though I'm not sure I do. Somehow I say I'll meet her outside later, by the path at the edge of the woods.

I I I I I I I

It's another momentous day in May, when the wind lifts the air in an ardent rush. It's warm enough to take my jacket off, and I do. I let it drop to the ground, and it's such a good sound, the leather hitting the dirt, a nice, thick thud, that I drop down on top of it. I stretch out, on the field behind school. Close my eyes. Unwind me. *Soothing* was Jane's word for the pond. I can't wait to get there—it's less than a mile away. Soothing, calling my name. I look up. It's the sun in my eyes.

"Hey," Jane says. Some people come up behind her, on the way to the woods.

"Hi," I say, squinting as I look toward the bright sky. The people pass.

"Such a great day, huh? Do you want to stay here for a while?" she says.

"Too much traffic for me." I stand.

"Okay, let's get to the pond, then. What's the name of it, anyway?" Her books are in a knapsack on her back. She's got her thumbs hooked into the front pockets of her jeans.

"There is no name," I say. "In my head I always just call it Quack Pond."

"Next stop, Quack Pond."

We start plodding down the dirt path until we're running. Too bad we can't fly, because that's what it feels like. We start to laugh and can't stop even after we get to the bottom of the hill. I can't run anymore because my sides are hurting. Not used to laughing, I guess. But Jane keeps going.

"Stop, stop!" I say, "please." I try to keep up, gulping air. I have no wind. Let the wind in.

"Only if you tell me something. Promise?" She turns, runs backward now, but slow, since we're in the woods.

"I give up."

"Say it!"

"I promise!" I say, and stop.

She whirls around. "Why do they call you Le Chien?"

"Oh, shit," I say.

"You promised! If you don't tell, that's the end, Virginia!" Jane tosses her knapsack to the ground.

"The end of what?"

"Don't try it; don't change the subject."

"Nice jacket," I say, and point to her motorcycle jacket. "Have I said that before? I mean it." And I do. I grab the knapsack from the ground. "So what's in here?"

"Look, you promised." She lurches for the knapsack, but I'm too quick.

"What's in here?" I say. "Secrets?"

"I don't keep secrets."

"Oh, no? What do you do—give them away?"

We both start to laugh.

"I'll make you a deal," I say, and toss her the knapsack.

"Hey, I didn't say anything about deals," Jane says. "But okay, Dunn, let me guess . . . You guys did a play in French class, and . . ."

I interrupt. "Don't bother guessing. It's stupid, really. . . . It's just that there was another Virginia in my class, so when we were getting renamed in French, Madame Audroue, the teacher, told me to open my French book and pick out a word. So there it was—*chien*. '*Chien*, merci!' said Madame. '*Les chiennes, le chien.* And so we shall call you Le Chien and avoid confusion with Virginie, *n'est-ce pas?*' And that's how I got to be called the dog. Humiliating enough?"

Jane is laughing. "It's kinda nice, I think."
"Sure it is. But I am not a dog. . . ."
"Not in this lifetime."
We walk.

"So did they do *Romeo and Juliet* in your old school?" I finally say.
" 'But soft! What light through yonder window breaks?' " Romeo, in the form of Jane, is before me.
We are leaving the woods now, coming to the paved road about a quarter of a mile from school. We have to cross that and then a field to get to the pond.
"Oh, how I go for that line, you know? But soft . . ."
"What do you think of the play?" I ask.
"Now that's a simple question," she says.

"Get this," I say. " 'The foundation of any romantic attachment is passion.' " I repeat Sanders' phrase.
"*Foundation?* Is love a building?"
I wish I'd thought of that. What *did* I think? Oh yeah, *attachment* is what stuck in my mind. The foundation part made no sense to me. We cross the road. We're almost there. But the play is stuck in my head. " 'Romeo come forth, thou fearful man. Affliction is enamor'd

of thy parts, and thou art wedded to calamity,' " I say. It's a phrase we read this morning.

Calamity. That line disturbs me. I shake my head, and when I stop, it feels like something starts to crack deep inside. What's going on?

I am beside her. Jane looks over. "What did you say?" Her voice is so soft, it breaks some window in me. Suddenly I'm in tears. "We think if we love somebody we'll live happily ever after—look! People are going to die even if you love them, they're just going to die!— Wedded to calamity!"

"I know," Jane says, her arm around me, so warm I lean into it without a thought. "We're almost there; let's get to the pond."

ı ı ı ı ı ı ı

The wind shudders through the water, and the bite-size swells tremble as they lap at the shore. There is a bunch of ducks skimming in circles, dipping their beaks beneath the surface of the pond.

"Are you okay, V?" Jane says. We sit by the edge, where there's a meager patch of sand, our bare feet in the warm water.

"I guess so," I say, actually calm. "Thanks." She calls me V, so easily, like she always has.

"We can talk about it, you know, if you want to."

"Anyone you know ever die?" I say.

"Not a person. But Barney did, my dog."

"You had a dog? I like his name. When?"

"Me too," she says. "It was about six months ago." Jane tosses a rock into the water and stares after the sinking noise. "But, you know, I was almost glad he did. He had arthritis in both hips. It was so bad he couldn't walk at the end. I had to carry him outside."

I think of Lucky in my arms. "Was he big?"

"No, a schnauzer."

"Really? My dog is small too, but he's a mutt. Are schnauzers good dogs?"

"Well, Barney was the best. And so cute. I miss him." She kicks the water.

"I bet," I say. "I know where you can get another dog, if you ever want to. Where I got mine."

"Oh, thanks. Maybe when I'm ready."

We look at the water and the ducks.

"I'm going to miss my dad," I say. I envision his empty slippers.

"Tell him, V. You know, Romeo and Juliet may have loved each other, but they didn't communicate very well. Now, the French writers, they know how to communicate."

"Like Rimbaud?" Did she say tell my father?

"Rimbaud's the best," she says, and smiles. It's as if she's never smiled before, because I can't take my eyes away from her face. When Jane looks over, the smile actually slams into me as I look back, but in such a pleasing way, I swear there's never been anything like it. How can I feel this way when I'm crying about my father?

"There's nobody like him," she says.

I choke. Does she know what I'm thinking too?

"Do you know his stuff?"

"Not much," I say.

"Well, he started writing when he was *ten* years old, and his first poem was published when he was sixteen. After school, he became a wanderer and a real bohemian. I've read that he lived in a state of filth, and that's because he was reading occult and 'immoral' literature—whatever that is—I haven't found out yet. He was rebelling against the bourgeois life he was surrounded by. But then he'd write these *beautiful* poems. Listen to this one," she says, and pulls the ragged book from her knapsack:

On blue summer nights I will go down the paths . . .
I will not speak, I will not think a thing,
But infinite love will rise in my soul,
And I will go far, so far, like a bohemian,
By nature, happy as if I had a girl.

"You know, the first time I read it, I thought it said, 'as if I *was* a girl,' but it's better this way, don't you think, V?"

| | |

What does she mean? I can't answer that question. She calls me V like we've known each other forever. Like we trust each other. What do I think? "Did you study him?" I finally say.

"Oh, no." She tosses another rock into the pond. "Both my parents teach French lit. They're going to start summer session at the college soon." She laughs. "That's why we're staying in that hideous house at Sagamore."

"Don't you like it there?"

"Sure, me and all the other robots."

We laugh. Then we're as quiet as the air. Maybe I will trust her.

"So what do you think about death, anyway?" I finally ask.

Jane doesn't even hesitate. "What I think these days is how sad you are and I wish there was something I could do."

I take a deep breath, and when I let it out, a piece of me seems to go with it. In the empty space is a new feeling. One that trembles, roaming and tender, that shakes my hands from the inside out. Who is Jane? I want to touch her, to make sure she's real.

landing

My dad is home.

Who said that? I did. A simple matter of hours passing has managed what was unthinkable just a few days ago. He's home. Isn't that amazing?

My dad's amazing. From gagging to crazy to walking out the door. A couple of nurses were standing in the hall, shaking their heads. "Sometimes they just close their eyes when they hear it—but will you take a look at *this* . . ." said one. And their heads actually wagged. "Looks like he's got plans, if you get me," said the other. Their wagging seemed to be shaking the disbelief out. They laughed almost like they were coughing, the weight of relief landing in the sound.

I heard and saw it all because I was walking behind my dad, Baby Teeth's hand in mine. Edward had Dad's suitcase and was thoughtful enough to carry it on his unaccompanied side, so it didn't smash into my leg. Wasn't that nice? My mother had one arm around my dad's bony shoulders. "Take your time, sweetheart," I heard her say. "There's no rush."
"You must be kidding," he said, and they actually laughed. "Get me out of here!"

My dad had refused to sit in the wheelchair that was required, for insurance reasons, to wheel patients beyond the hospital entryway, to the outside. To the world. "I'm no longer a patient," he said to the attendant who had appeared and recited these rules as we were leaving the room. "I'll find my own way out, thank you," my dad said.

The attendant, with a helpless shrug of his white-coated shoulders, began to follow us, leaning on the handles of the empty, rolling wheelchair. Though it took my

dad forever to walk, we eventually reached the main
exit. He had begun to push with one hand against the
yellow wall to create momentum.

I remembered that feeling, that pushing. I did that as
a kid—against a wall, or against the ground at the
beginning of a race—maybe to catch up with somebody,
maybe just hoping nothing could stop me. My breath
snagged when I saw my dad's pushing hand. Then
I got the hiccups. Edward started laughing. Then
Baby Teeth started. I had to beg them to stop because
laughing and choking simultaneously was agony.
It almost had me crying, exactly what I was trying to
avoid.

My mother made a big homecoming meal of Dad's favorites, steak and new red potatoes, sautéed string
beans, white onions in her special cream sauce. She
was opening and closing oven doors as soon as we
arrived home. "I was hoping it would make you hungry," she said to Dad. Since she had prepared everything earlier in the day, the stuff just waited for
us.

Edward helped my dad get situated at the dining-room
table, and that took as much time as it did for me to
take Lucky outside for his walk and then back inside
to his waiting dinner bowl. My dad's so skinny, it looks
like if he even thinks about walking his legs might

break. But they made it from the car to the dining-room chair. Edward's hand under my dad's elbow is a good support, Dad had said.

At the table he began to ask all kinds of questions— had Baby Teeth lost any molars, and how was Edward's car running? Let's see Lucky's leg and when was the cast coming off? I began to wonder if this was really my father, because these were the kinds of questions he had never asked.

My old father was always talking about lawn mower engine sizes or how old the pine trees would have to be before they could act as a privacy fence between us and the house next door. My mother had to remind him of stuff like birthdays and Baby Teeth's stubborn bicuspids. As he sat there, my dad actually turned red from all those questions. My mother had to tell him to slow down.

So there we were in the early American dining room, surrounded by polished, gleaming wood; everything in this house was made of wood, the room usually reserved for holidays or company. In a way, we were company. We were the new Dunns, the downhill ones, the after-the-news-keep-a-stiff-upper-lip-that's-the-Irish-way Dunns.

I I I

And what was wrong with me? I was suddenly filled with a terrible urge to laugh. I knew if I did that the sound would be as high-pitched as a siren, but more bitter. I could taste it. Then I began to experience that crawling feeling, the one that lifted me out of my chair and sent me floating to the ceiling. There I was, looking down at the good-smelling, gleaming dinner table. I saw everyone happy and relieved, and then I lost my appetite.

The person on the ceiling wondered if this was really my father, or whether, because so much had happened, he had turned into someone else. Shut up, I said to myself, it's just vertigo. I'm dizzy. It's just anxiety. I floated down.

I slid my hand under the table and fed bits of steak to Lucky, the begging expert, who waited with his head against my leg, chin on my knee. Lucky ate more than anyone. I noticed that though all of us were acting very carefree, heaping food onto plates and pouring gravy, no one was actually eating.

Dad must've noticed too, because he cleared his throat and said, "Let's make the best of it, okay? It's a great meal and we're all together." Now, that was my *old* demanding dad talking. But who was the new one? And what would I say to him? I looked at the skinny, gray person in my dad's chair. His jaw and cheekbones stuck out like they were too big for his face.

"Chew every bite one hundred times!" Baby Teeth said, each hand wound so tightly around her knife and fork, she wouldn't be dropping any utensils at this meal.

"That's a fine idea," my mother agreed, her eyes as bright as the chandelier above our heads.

"For digestion," Baby Teeth added. Her voice was normal.

"That's what they say." My dad nodded.

"Mrs. Engel said so. . . ." Mrs. Engel was the grammar school librarian. But something was not right. Baby Teeth's knuckles paled as she gripped the silver.

"No plucking mole hairs either," Baby Teeth added, in a smaller voice. Edward gagged on a mouthful of onions. I wanted to disappear. I remembered one of the fifth-grade teachers who had had a mole on her chin, but I couldn't recall her name. Oh, yes, Mrs. Angel. I looked uncertainly at my sister, waiting.

"That's right," Baby Teeth said, tapping a potato with her knife. "It can give you cancer."

"Rachel!" My mother's fork clattered against her plate, slid into her gravy.

We all looked at my sister. For no reason, I thought the chandelier might crash down onto the table.

"Let her," my father said, wiping his hand over his brow.

"Did you know that, Daddy?" Baby Teeth asked.

"I didn't know that, no."

"You don't have cancer, do you, Daddy?" Baby Teeth's knife was rapping against her plate. She didn't notice.

"No, honey, I don't." My father grabbed the white napkin from his lap and wiped behind his neck with it.

"We're at the table," my mother said. I could hear her teeth clench.

"It's *okay*." My father looked only at my sister's plate, and Baby Teeth finally became aware that her hand was connected to the rapping noise. It stopped.

"I guess I have something worse than that, honey."

My mother twisted in her chair, but she said nothing.

"And right now it's okay that I do, because I'm here. We get to be together. That's okay, isn't it?"

When I managed to yank my eyes from their hold on my shriveling, cold potatoes, I saw that my dad's eyes were wet.

"So you're staying home now?" Baby Teeth asked.

My dad nodded.

When Baby Teeth nodded, her hands finally relaxed, and her knife and fork tumbled to the tablecloth.

"It's real good you're here, Dad," Edward said, eyes as thick as the milk in his glass.

When my father smiled, his face looked like it was made of wax. "Thanks, Ed. Just a little worse for wear is all."

Nobody said anything more, so we tried to eat. And then we stopped trying. It was obvious my dad couldn't eat right now; he'd managed to cut up and swallow only a few soft onions, so nobody else ate either. Baby Teeth dropped her fork again and let it stay dropped. I reached for my water glass. It was hard to swallow. It wasn't what he said, but what he meant. We're all together now. Soon we won't be.

After dinner we watched old home movies. It was Dad's idea, after he changed into his favorite robe, the brown one with the patches on the elbows, and his old slippers. Even Edward watched. If the projector didn't whir noisily as the motor spun, I'd swear the only thing anybody could hear would be the way my heart pounded. The dusty reels came out of the closet, and we sprawled across the living-room floor to watch. My parents sat on the couch behind us. My father usually made the movies on holidays, so as a result he didn't appear in much footage. I'd never noticed that before—his absence—and when I saw it, even my eyes felt empty. As if he were already gone.

The rest of us, in successive years, walked through the front door, sometimes in matching holiday outfits, and waved at the camera. We looked like a happy family.

And as we watched, we laughed as if we were. My mother laughed, whooping louder than anybody, mostly at herself, because each time the camera had focused on her, she had fled. When it caught her, she was blushing, embarrassed. She looked like Baby Teeth.

Between reels, my mother disappeared into the pantry. I could hear the ice tumble into her glass. Lucky rolled around on his back, doing his dog twist, ecstatic that people were on the floor with him. I scratched his belly. After a while my ears began to ring, I realized, unaccustomed to all this noise and commotion in my own house.

Baby Teeth eventually turned the lights back on, and Edward rewound the last reel of film. When my father said "I've had a good life because of all of you" is when everything suddenly stopped moving. Edward forgot to shut the machine off, and all we heard was the film flapping as it spun into a chaotic mess all over the floor.

Lucky barked as if the film were alive, which Baby Teeth seemed to find the most hilarious moment of her life. Then all of us were laughing. We only stopped when we saw that Baby Teeth had begun to cry.

welcome
hurry

My life is in a slithering heap on the living-room floor. The film is everywhere. Too bad I can't toss my thoughts into the pile, since they seem to be heaped in my head. Too bad I can't just take a broom and sweep up the big, slippery mess. What can I do?

I call Jane. Even though I worry it's too late at night, at least it's Friday. It's Friday, right? She answers on the first ring.

"Where have you been?" she says. "I was hoping you'd call."

"My dad's home. We watched all the old home movies."

"Are you okay?"

I don't say anything. That's a good question.

"I wish I was there," she says.

"So do I."

"Look in the mirror."

"What?" I say. I worry.

"Go look in a mirror. Can the phone reach?"

"Hang on." I'm in the den. Just me and my snoring dog. I open the closet door and pull the phone over. "Okay," I say, "there I am."

"What do you see?"

"Me." I feel ridiculous.

"What about you?"

"My eyes always get green when I cry."

"They do? So it's all emotional, huh? What else?"

I stare at myself, what I do every morning, always wanting to see if anything has gone crooked overnight. There I am again. It's true my eyebrows are not even. They're as lopsided as my brain feels tonight. "Well, I look like my dad." Do I say that?

| | |

"You do? What does he look like?" Jane says.

"What? Oh, tall, and dark. But pale. His eyes, though, are incredible—I bet they could see through walls. That probably sounds stupid, but I always thought that."

"So he must be really good-looking," Jane says.

I laugh a very small laugh. I'm describing my former father, not the frail version who's home now.

"See anything else?"

"No." I can't tell her more.

"You're still in one piece, right?" Jane says.

"I think so . . . except for my brains, ha, ha."

"Yuk, yuk, yourself. And what you probably don't see is that surprised look on your face."

I blink at the mirror. "What?"

"The one that's always there."

"I don't feel surprised," I say. My eyes are swollen. I feel empty from crying.

"Probably because you're always full of what surprises you," Jane says.

"What does it look like?" I say. She can't mean these puffy cheeks.

"Like you can't believe you're really here."

"That's what I look like?" I *am* surprised by that.

"That's what I love best about you. Can we meet in the morning and go to the pond?"

"Sure," my voice says, my lips crooked as I talk. How does she think these things?

"Meet me at ten. End of your driveway."

As I look in the mirror, I do look like my father. The flesh strains at the edges of my mouth, the shadows beneath my eyes. I know I've thought before if he dies I'll die too, but I'm scared. His eyes look so unbelievably hollow now, as if they can't focus on anything *outside*, no, only on what's *inside*, and it looks dark in there. It scares me. I didn't say that to Jane. Or that my heart beats so much now I can hear it all the time. It keeps reminding me that I'm alive. I don't want to die.

ı ı ı ı ı ı

In the morning I feel unnaturally calm, like there's a version of me in the back of my head watching the rest of me. It's not the floating, anxious me. It's me, but detached from myself, like pieces of metal, maybe car parts. This is a new one. V, the busted muffler. Oh, delight. As we sit by the pond, I wonder about this, how many versions of themselves a person can become before the face in the mirror is unrecognizable. Until those uneven eyebrows or crooked lips are so distant they turn into a memory, even while they're being looked at.

ı ı ı

"It doesn't make sense that I'll die," I say.

Jane pretends to check for a fever, hand on my forehead. "You're not dead yet."

"Maybe I am."

"You mean I'm talking to a ghost?"

"See you at my funeral. Will you come?" I say.

"When do I RSVP?"

"And for a eulogy you would say what?"

"I don't know you well enough," Jane says. "Eileen should do it, I think, but you two are on the outs or something, is that it?"

Eileen. She would only run away.

We're lying inches apart, in the grass by the edge of the water. The grass is swaying in the mild breeze.

"Look at the ducks," I say, pointing across the pond, wanting to push Eileen from my mind. There's a small bunch standing along the shoreline across the water. They're so still, their beaks lowered, they look almost as if they're praying. It's unusual that they're all on land, not a solitary one skimming circles in the water. The pond is also still, just an occasional lap of water disappearing into the sand.

It begins to feel unusual that Jane is lying so close to me. And then I have an even more unusual thought. I want her to lie closer. Inside me would be good. If only we could get rid of these clumsy bodies and dissolve into each other. The way water disappears into sand.

I I I

I don't know if I've ever felt anything more strongly
than the feeling that we belong together. It comes in a
rush that swerves in a welcome hurry through my arms
and legs. It's so strong I feel connected to the ground,
as if a hushed, wet hand of wind has slipped along and
slid inside me. I'm so full and the feeling is so strong
I think that if I move, I'll burst. I want to look at Jane,
to see if she can feel what's happening. That's when
she kisses me. Her entire body and everything I wonder
about in her seems to roll onto my lips as she kisses
me. Then she kisses me again. It's beyond dissolving.

just
by
being
there

I don't know the name for the feeling that's crawling inside me, but I know what it is. It was very strong with Grant Sullivan, who I didn't always hate the way I do now. The truth is, I used to like him. Much more than I want to admit. But the truth is so important now, and I don't know why that is either. I have to tell it. I feel like if I don't tell the truth about everything, I'll die. If I can't make somebody understand what I feel,

I'll disintegrate into the air. My eyes will close. My mouth will shut. My life will vanish. I'm too young to die.

The truth can sometimes wake somebody. Earlier than the birds, I am awake. It's Sunday morning. I get up and wander into the kitchen. I see Edward through the window, his head under the hood of the Plymouth. I walk outside.

"It's me," I say to the visible part of his ponytail.

"Is it you?" he replies.

"Can't sleep."

"I could have told you that." He lifts his head to look at me. "You look like shit," he says.

"Thanks, Wadface. I can always rely on you for the facts." My blunt brother. Well, it's not a *bad* quality. It doesn't leave any room for confusion, at least. "I'm worried," I say. That's the truth.

"I know." He's serious.

I look directly into my brother's eyes. They are still clear.

"Gonna have to glue up," he says, backing away from the engine. "Stick around."

"Sure." 'Glue up'? What was this new language? He drops the rag he's holding and grabs a cigarette from a pack in his shirt pocket.

"It's pretty obvious Dad's not long," he mumbles, cigarette dangling from his lips.

I hear a grunt. It's me, trying to say something. We haven't said anything *out loud* about my dad until now. Edward just takes a long drag off his cigarette and waits.

"I don't know what we're going to do," I say. It's so vague but it's true, and my eyes are blurring with tears. I don't know what to say.

Edward grabs me in a quick hug.

"The thing is," he says, "I want you to know . . . is that, soon as I'm eighteen, I'm gone too." He won't look at me, reaches instead for the rag and twists the cap off a bottle of 5W-30.

"What are you talking about?" Is he telling me he's sick? Did he hug me?

"I'm going into the army; I'm all joined up. Going to study engines, but nobody knows. I want to keep it that way for now, because there's enough going on around here, don't you think?" When Edward grins, his ears redden.

"You?" is all I manage, spluttering now, like the oil as it oozes into the casing beneath the hood.

"Like I said. So it looks like everything around here is going to be fallin' on you." The grin vanishes.

"But Edward, the army? What's falling?" The sky? My life into pieces?

"You know what I mean . . . Mom will be a wreck."
I don't know who's more surprised when I say, "But you can't leave. I mean, what will I do without you?"

"You'll be okay. You're tougher than she is."

I look at him. "That's not what I mean—*anyone's* tougher than she is—she's already a wreck, don't you know that?"

He watches me. "Maybe. But you, you can do anything you want to with all those brains." He's so serious I can't stand it.

I shake my head. "Edward, I want to ask you something."

He just nods.

"Did you quit taking drugs?"

He nods again.

"How come?"

"Mind over matter—you can figure that one out."

I try to wipe the tears away from my eyes, but when I do, more surface. "Oh, no," I say.

"What?"

"They'll cut off all your hair."

"That was the hardest part about deciding to join."

How horrible it is to try to grow up. We can't stop laughing. And then I hug him. He whispers, "Make sure you take care of Baby Teeth, okay?"

Eventually, I walk back into the house, my head spinning. But there's Lucky—tilting, limping miracle dog, tail wagging at the door. I grab him and kiss him all over his delighted head. I tell him next week his cast is coming off and we'll parade around town. I tell him, don't worry, I'll find that miserable green VW. I tell him I love him. Lucky's not going anywhere.

ı ı ı ı ı ı ı

Jane is standing at the end of my driveway. It's still morning and I'm strolling around the yard with Lucky, and there she is. Standing on one of the big white rocks that surround the place. She smiles that smile when she sees me and lifts her arms like she's going to bow. Like it's a performance.

"What are you doing here?" I say, noticing the burning feeling start inside.

"I wanted to see you," she answers.

"You could've called. I can't believe you're here." I don't know why I'm being so mean.

"I know I could've called," she says. I've never seen the way her lower lip juts out when her feelings get hurt.

"Well, I guess we can go for a walk," I finally manage, not able to look at her again. "Wait, let me get him inside."

"He's adorable. Can I meet him?"

I ignore her. "I'll be right back."

We start walking. I can't say anything. Just seeing her feet next to mine is too much. If she brushes against me the way she always does, I think I'll break. We

walk in silence before she finally says, "Virginia, tell
me what's wrong."
"I don't know." That's true. All I know is that if I look
at her the tears that are holding on to my eyes will burst
out, and the wind is back, but rushing through me now
in a cold and dreadful way. I am stuck, but stuck inside
myself. What is the feeling? What terrible thing is
gnawing at me? Then something happens.

My legs, which are still miraculously walking, moving
along like they aren't connected to me, moving as heavily and clumsily as if they are tree stumps, trip. Trip
over a blade of grass, and I fall, tumbling forward as
though the world has just tipped over. I trip with my
arms like clock hands careening around a clockface
with time going so impossibly fast that days pass before
my eyes as I fall. And then I'm on the ground.

Jane is next to me before I know it, and all I can do
is laugh. Suddenly, the ground, the sidewalk, the
stricken look on Jane's face are all indescribably funny. She looks at me, wondering, I imagine, if I have
lost my mind. Then she catches it. She's laughing,
and we can't stop at all, not if someone threatened to
shoot us, our voices filling the morning air. She holds
me just as tightly as I hold her as we reel in the grip
of this new spell we're under. The laughter, like
wind, finally stops.

| | |

"You look just like you did the first time I saw you," she says.

"When was that?"

"The day I registered at school—it was in the hall."

"You saw me that day?"

"Of course I did, V. Didn't you see me?"

"Yes." Of course *I* did, but I didn't know she'd seen me.

"What did I look like?" I ask.

"Like a lost kid at a parade."

Then she tells me she's supposed to be at the Dairy Barn, getting a quart of milk. We don't say good-bye. We just look at each other. Why not? Why? I'm standing on the empty road.

There are too many questions. The crawling feeling is back. At this moment it's fear that crawls through me. It shakes my hands from the inside out. I have a certain feeling about Jane. It seems it's one I've always had, only I never knew it. Who cares if it's possible, it's true. What's the feeling? I'm still standing on the road.

After yesterday at the pond with Jane, after making out with Jane, I wanted to run away. Last night, as I lay in bed, all I could do was feel her mouth on mine. It's the same feeling I have when I see her sweep her head of beautiful hair through the air or watch that undulating walk of hers.

Except it's part of me now, as I stand on the road. It's on my mouth and I can taste it. The most amazing feeling I've ever had. If there was anything that didn't exist when she was kissing me, when I was kissing her, because we got so tangled up together, it was time. We kissed forever. The last thing I wanted to do was stop. And then we did stop, I guess, but I don't know when. And then we looked at each other. It was hard to look into her eyes, but it was even harder to tear my eyes from her as we said good-bye. I couldn't stop feeling the feeling.

But when I saw her today, the last place I wanted to be was near her. I don't know why. When something broke in me and I kept laughing even when the laughing was over so she wouldn't take her arms away, the hands that reached so instantly for me when I fell. I wished she would kiss me again, even though we were in the middle of the road.

I didn't care that the entire world could've seen. Nothing else mattered. And what was all the other stuff about? The anger, I mean. Why was I acting so mean when I first saw her on my driveway? Why did I feel that she was asking something impossible of me just by being there? Is it because I'm afraid she'll leave too? I'm afraid to ask myself one question in particular, but I know I have to, because it's digging a hole inside me. Do I love her? I mean, do I love her?

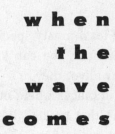

when
the
wave
comes

Like everybody else in the world, it seemed, we had
headed toward the ocean. It was at least five years ago,
during a dry, sweltering August. Ours and a million
other cars inched by the BEACH signs along the highway.
The car was packed with sand chairs, beach umbrellas,
and fishing poles.

l l l

Wadbreath was sprawled out on the backseat, and my sister and I were all the way in the back of the old red station wagon. I was searching for the bag that held the hard-boiled eggs and giving Baby Teeth a bird lecture.

"There are at least ninety species of sparrows recorded in North America. You can look at them and wonder how they stay alive, they're so small. But sparrows are able to live in places where other birds find it hard to survive. Isn't that great?" I loved knowing stuff like this. My dad had told me about the birds, in just this way. That's how I remembered, why I said it this way. "Do you know how many ninety is?"

"What?" my sister said. She had wanted to sit in the front with my mother and, for spite, pretended she couldn't hear me. But when Baby Teeth pretended in this way, she wanted everyone to know. "WHAT? WHAT? WHAT?"

"Stop it," my mother said.

I assumed my mother was talking to my sister, whose dreadful attitude was, to my mother's mind, I'm sure, infecting the whole gang. My mother didn't like it when we were finally all together and everybody didn't pretend to be overjoyed. I have to remind myself that this was five years ago.

"Only some sparrows are good singers. A canary is a sparrow; did you know that? Canaries have terrific voices." I could still smell the eggs, but I couldn't find them.

"Virginia, did you hear me?"

"We're almost there," my father called, to no one in particular, but happily. He was always in a good mood when we were in the car going somewhere. When we really traveled, to places we'd never been, like zoos or lakes, we always got lost.

My father refused to look at a map, though my mother's hands always held one during those journeys. She'd point out that he'd inevitably taken a wrong turn, and he'd ignore her. It was like he was driving in a dream, making up the directions as he went along. Eventually his smile would fade, unable, I guess, to sustain itself against my mother's complaints.

"Will you stop ruining the trip before we even get there?" he'd say, and finally grab the map.

"I just don't want to get there tomorrow," she'd answer, head turned smugly to the window.

It was my opinion that he wanted to get lost.

At least he knew the way to the beach. After parking in one of the numbered "fields," each holding hundreds of cars, it seemed to take forever to walk to the shore. Especially weighed down with beach stuff. Everybody squinted against the immense summer sun. It was ninety-eight degrees and not even noon. A real scorcher, that's what the deep voice on the radio

had said while we drove. I never found the eggs.
That's because Wadnod, who later confessed, had se-
cretly eaten them all.

A storm was expected later that day, and the ocean
confirmed the voice on the radio. The waves were impossibly huge and wild. The water was not blue that
day, but white. White with the whipping sea spray and
breaking waves.

Baby Teeth begged my father to put her down as they
stood at the edge of the water. Her tears made it clear
that she was afraid. I was scared too. But I was also
drawn to it, in the same way I was pulled toward sleep
when I closed my eyes. The embracing waves, the floating surrender. The problem with the ocean was that it
was just too big. It could swallow somebody.

Because I knew that in the ocean were tremendous
monsters with vicious teeth. Just looking at the water,
I felt the feeling that washed over me as I lay in bed
at night, when I could still think but my thoughts were
dunking and floating at the same time. When life was
bobbing behind my eyes in a haphazard, sprawling way.
The spray of the surf as it flew through the scorching
air was a cool relief against my skin. But when I looked
out at the ocean and was struck by how dangerous
it was, everything inside me seemed to clatter, like
breaking shells.

I I I

My dad finally put Baby Teeth down. She dropped her tube into the sand. "Not me," she said, and ran as fast as her petrified three-year-old legs would carry her.

"Do you want to go in with me?" he asked, his grinning face looming above me.

"I don't know." The surf was so cool, but the waves were so big.

"Just hold my hand," he offered, "and when the wave comes, we dive under. Just hold on to my hand."

Though I couldn't tell him, I knew that he knew I was scared. He kept smiling and nodding at me the way I'd seen people look at babies. But I couldn't say anything. I wanted to go, even though I was scared. Just me and my dad. When I finally reached out my hand for his, I think I stopped breathing. I had just seen *Moby Dick*, and Gregory Peck had died a brutal death in that movie, strapped to the back of the whale. I knew how to swim, that much I knew, but not in a wild ocean. Not in an ululating sea like this.

A lot of whooping noises and splashing usually followed my father as he went into the water. 'Getting acquainted,' he called it. But not today. Today we stood as still as telephone poles.

"Ready?" he said. "Just hold on." And, without waiting for an answer, tugged at my hand, dragging me into the deep. The terror was under my feet, where there was nothing. Nothing but the swirl of my mind, spinning in the grip of my daddy's hand. Just hold on, I told myself.

The white waves crashed around us, brutal and spitting. And what fools we were, rushing to meet them! I must've opened my mouth in horror, or to say something, because suddenly it was full of salt, burning, when my father yelled, "Dive!" and let go of my hand.

I saw him disappear into the monstrosity of the sea at the same instant I was struck by it, tumbling me over and over in a ridiculous, unending somersault. I rolled and spun, the sea filling my mouth and ears, my eyes, wide open.

Finally I hit the shore. The sand ran inside my bathing suit, into my ears, finding the hidden folds of skin like biting teeth. I hit the shore in a heap. My eyes stung from salt that cut like glass. Then the tears were gone. In their place for anyone to see was a new terror. My father.

"You didn't dive!" I heard him say. "If you don't dive, you sink, you get pulled under! You end up like this." I saw his hand above me as I sprawled across the sand. His mouth was wide, just like the sea, and spread into a grin.

"You said hold on." I was on my knees, wiping the sand from my unsmiling face.

"I dove under, and then when the wave passed, I could stand," my father said. "I thought you were with me on this."

"But you *said* hold on." I hated him. "I thought you were with *me*."

"But you can't hold on *and* dive. You need *both* hands to dive."

"Why didn't you say so before?" What I hated the most was that I had *believed* him. "You lied to me."

"No, please." He laughed and reached to help me stand up. "I didn't lie. I just thought you would know . . . but you . . . it's my fault."

I would not let him help me and twisted from his grasp. "But you know what, V? Next time, you won't forget."

I might *never* forget, that's what I knew. I didn't know what else I'd remember.

roaring

The bloody sheets are still on his bed. When we left the hospital last Friday, Edward moved into the guest room upstairs at home and Dad took my brother's room on the first floor. It was obvious that my father wouldn't be climbing any stairs. We lived this new way for all of two days. One weekend. Today is Monday, my dad is back in the hospital, and the bloody sheets are still on his bed.

||||

Last week, following Thursday's dreadful scene full of fever and rash and delirium, Dr. Sweeney and the hematologist appeared in the room. They said there was nothing else they could do if my dad refused to try the plethora of experimental medications that was available. The plethora? My dad was not experiencing any active infections at this time. Nobody said anything about a cure.

"So I'll go home," my dad said. If you feel you'll be more comfortable there. Private-duty nurses, hospice, alternatives were available. They were very careful about how they said all this, but every word was exaggerated. *Alternatives* blared loud as a car horn. My dad said, "If I'm going to die, I'll do it at home." That's when the doctors blinked, like my dad was a bully tossing sand in their eyes, and they looked away.

But nobody said he was going to hemorrhage. Or that he would sleep all weekend and then his blood would stop clotting and start spilling out all over the sheets.

And my dad said, not like this. I'm not going like this, covered in blood; he said it. He had just woken up. It was this morning. Both blankets, since he was always cold, were soaked in blood. We all stood there, gaping at the sight, as if *we* had been wounded. My dad groaned. That's when I grabbed the blankets and my mother grabbed my dad's robe. Edward ran outside to start the car. Baby Teeth had already left for school, which was a relief. We rushed back to the hospital.

 I   I   I   I   I   I

That was this morning, all the blood. And now it's afternoon. I'm walking along the street trying to remember and forget everything at once. I don't want to forget anything about my dad. I don't want to remember this morning. The sun is shining into my eyes in such a way that I'm blind if I tilt my head. I even want to remember that. It's Monday afternoon, after school. I wish I could forget how heavy those blankets were. I went to school today.

I saw Jane in school and told her that I was going straight back to the hospital with Edward this afternoon. That was a lie. I'm going home to meet Edward and Baby Teeth first. When I get home, what I'm going to do is take the bloody sheets off the bed. I don't want Baby Teeth to see that.

What I told Jane is true enough. The real truth is that I just can't stand the thought of being near her today. When I'm with her, I feel like stuff is being dragged out of me. As I'm being emptied, another part of me fills with worry. Will she kiss me again? When?

 I   I   I

I wonder if it matters to her as much as it does to me.
She said she wanted to do everything once. Like Rimbaud. Rimbaud wanted to do everything once. Is that
all? I don't really know what she meant by that. "Nobody's serious when they're seventeen." That's another
Rimbaud line. What about fifteen, I wonder. What's
that supposed to be like? How serious are we now? I
read that Rimbaud stopped writing when he was nine-
teen. He was "disillusioned." Why? It's hard to find
the true meaning in things. Especially what Jane
means. I can't wait to be with her, but then I can't
stand it when I am.

So I walk along, blinded by the day, when a car races
by at a phenomenal speed, the radio blaring impossibly
loud. It stops me, foot in the air. When I hear it, I
want to remember how it came out of nowhere, into my
thoughts at the moment I was thinking about Jane,
practically blind. Even though I can't see it yet, I want
it to mark the moment, like a gunshot marks the start
of a race. I want to remember this moment in ten years
because it seems so important, the ground vibrating
beneath my feet as I stand, marking. Perhaps in ten
years I will know what it means. So what is this feeling? It's not longing for the past; that's nostalgia.
What about the opposite of nostalgia? Longing for the
present? But if I'm not already in the present, where
can I be?

I I I

That's when I hear the roaring. Initially I think it must be the noise inside my own head. The noise of confusion. Then I hear a big slam. My head is bent into the blind angle, so I can't see anything at all. I jerk reflexively at the roaring. The slamming car door. I look up. The green VW. THE GREEN VW. The murderous Lucky-wrecking car. Outside that door is Eileen. The car roars away.

"Hey, V." Eileen tries to smile. "Saw you by accident."

"What! Whose car is that?" It *is* my head that's roaring.

"Listen, I know it's been a while, too long, I know, but we really need to talk." Eileen's eyes have widened as she looks at me.

"Whose car is that?"

"Look. I didn't know what happened." She also looks ready to run, her legs bent forward, heels off the sidewalk.

Like an animal, my mind says. "Who's driving that car?" I say.

"I can't believe it myself, V. I'm just getting a ride home and suddenly Grant is telling me everything about some ground-zero morning—you know, like *bad*—and a dog got hit and I say 'What, you mean V's Lucky?' and he begs me not to tell you—" She finally takes a breath.

"Stop!" I say. "What are you talking about?" The words sound like they're coming from the ground, not anywhere near my mouth. It's all so far away. "Sulli-

van was there? *Whose* car is it, Eileen? Please?"
"Shit, V." She stops, stares at the sidewalk. "Grant."

"That's *Sullivan's* car?" Ground zero? Did I hear that?
"It's his father's car, but he didn't mean it. Lucky came
out of nowhere. He really, really didn't mean it."
Eileen's heel kicks the ground.
"Sullivan . . . How do you know what he meant?" Something's rumbling beneath my words, like a train slowing down.
"I know because he just told me; what do you think,
he's some kind of killer? We just passed you and he
just told me."
"In Sullivan's car? You?" Why am I asking these imbecile questions? It's like my brain is slowing down.
Out of nowhere, she said.
"I was getting a ride, V, 'cause I missed the bus, and
you know how I hate to walk alone." Eileen starts to
whine. A picture flashes behind my eyes. In my mind
I kick her.

I shake my head and look down the road, after the
car. I can't believe this. Why not? It's not true.
"Why? Why did he wait so long? Why didn't he tell
me?"
"Are you kidding? He's scared of you. He says you hate
him." She's leaning forward. She's too tall to be a
liar.
"Sullivan is scared of me?"

"That's what he said, V." Those eyes, like puddles, so unlike Eileen.

"What?" My head hurts. Why did Sullivan ask me where Eileen was? And why does Eileen want to believe *him?*

"You're lying," I finally say.

"What did you say?"

"You've been lying to me for weeks. Every time I see you with that stupid hat on, it reminds me. Where is the ratty thing today, anyway?" I say. "I have news for you, Eileen. I just figured out where *you* were the day Lucky got hit. So *that's* why you've been such a nasty bitch—because you feel so bad for taking off when it happened, is that it? You didn't come to *my* place that day. Did you jump on the bus? Is that it? Is that it?"

Eileen's eyes are wet. "I don't know what you're talking about, but you have incredible nerve, calling me a liar. And *so* sorry you don't like my hat, like you are the fashion plate of the universe!"

"So you saw the whole Lucky accident, and you ran away. You've known for weeks . . . That's it, isn't it, why you've been acting like such a jerk? Why you've been avoiding me?"

Eileen straightens up. When she does, she's taller than me. I've always hated that. "You're the jerk, Virginia. I wasn't even there. I went to the dentist that morning; don't you remember? I wasn't even near the bus stop.

Don't you remember? Loretta told me. Loretta was
there, on the bus. I called you from school, V, as soon
as I knew. *You* didn't go to school that day." Her eyes
fill, and Eileen starts crying. "I called you the second
I heard. You were so upset I didn't know what to say.
Don't you remember that, you jerk?"

I do. I remember. Sprawled across the floor the day
Lucky got slammed, shaking so bad I couldn't hold the
phone, I couldn't talk. Just before that horrible conversation with my mother. Something inside me drops,
and I start crying too, standing on the sidewalk. "I'm
sorry—I forgot. I forgot you called. I thought you just
left. He asked me where you were."
"Who asked you?" Eileen says, hugging me.
"Sullivan."
"You're kidding. What? What's wrong with him?" She
looks down the road, wipes her eyes. "And you thought
I did? I can't believe it. What's wrong with him?"
As I look at her, her eyes are no longer wet, but they're
not the same. "You tell me," I say.

r u s h

I remember the sheets. "Listen, I have to go."
"Do you have to go *now?* I really need to talk to you."
Eileen looks at me. "Oh, it's your dad, isn't it? I'm sorry, V."
I just nod. Maybe that's enough communication for one day, I think, since I feel all weak—even my ears are weak, as the sound of Eileen's voice wobbles in—like

I might crumble into an irreparable pile of bones if I'm faced with any more *truth*.

"I'll call you later."

"You what?" I say. Part of me doesn't believe those words, since I haven't heard them in so long.

"There's some other stuff I have to tell you," Eileen says.

"You mean it?" Another part of me really wants to believe her.

"More than anything."

But maybe, some other part says, it's stuff I don't want to hear. Maybe my ears *are* tired.

| | | | | | |

Nobody else is home yet. I have time to wash the sheets, the blankets. But wait—where's Lucky? Not in his waiting-to-go-out spot by the door. Why not? I call him. Nothing. He's in front of Edward's bedroom door. He's chewing at his cast—there are white bits littering the carpet. Oh, poor dog. At least the cast is coming off in a few days. "Somebody around here hire a guard dog?" I say in my special canine voice. He growls.

I stop walking toward him. "Are you growling?" Yes, he is. He's never done that. "What's wrong?" I ask. Then I realize—it's the blood.

My voice starts out normal. "It's only me, Puppyhead." My hand is in slow motion, reaching for the door. "If you bite me, I'll lose my mind. Promise." It's a whisper. Lucky barks sharply as he rises and shakes himself out as if he's fled the driving rain. He limps away. "So," I say as my hand grasps the doorknob, "animals go crazy too."

When the door opens, I understand. The air itself is an anchor, weighed down with the thick stench of dried blood. My throat closes. My nostrils burn as if the air itself is burning. What smells like this?

If metal burned, it would be like this. But no. Metal is cold. A dreadful edge, as if I've bitten something sharp and bitter, like a rotten pepper, wells up in my eyes. It's the memory of the morning Lucky got hit. This morning my dad's blankets were the brightest red. This afternoon they're a dark, streaking brown. This morning the blood was warm. Now it looks like rust.

I don't want to see this. The hot shock rushes through my limbs. I go numb. This is somebody else's life. Stop—there must be a reason I'm here. But I don't want to see this. But I don't want Baby Teeth to see it even more. Okay. Before I know it, I roll it all into a big heap, I race through the hall, and throw it all down the basement stairs. I race down the stairs, spill detergent into the washing machine. I squeeze the stuff inside and shut the lid. I can breathe again.

| | |

I walk around the basement, shaking myself, just the way Lucky did, trembling my way back to life. The machine sloshes as it spins—it sounds like boots in a deep puddle. I notice that my mother has added more boxes to the piles of stuff she keeps everywhere. She can't throw anything away.

I see some photo albums sticking out of a box. I lift one from the pile, and the faded black leather crumbles into uneven pieces. I open the book and see pictures of my mother as a kid. I think I've seen them before, among the piles in the den cabinet, but as I turn the page, I don't recognize them.

In one picture, my mother and her sister are sitting on the steps of their Brooklyn brownstone. I've been there—it's Pop's old house. I recognize it by the building's faded brick. They're wearing black dresses and little black shoes. And both of them are wet, their long dark hair soaked and stringy around their shoulders. My mother is maybe ten years old. When is this? I keep looking. There's something wrong here. It's raining. Why are they sitting outside in the rain with no umbrellas? They look like the most miserable kids in Brooklyn.

I hear the phone ring upstairs. The washing machine spins. Good. Where are my siblings? I run up the stairs to answer. It's my mother.

"Virginia, Dad's better. The hemorrhaging's stopped—
for now."

"Great! What"—I'm out of breath—"what do you mean,
for now?"

She pauses. "All those drugs! Nobody can predict
anything."

"So are the doctors there? Is Dad awake?"

"No . . . the drugs . . ." Her voice trails off. "Is Edward
there yet?" She pauses. How can silence be like a
storm?

I finally say, "Not yet." There's something wrong, and
she's not telling.

"Okay, everybody stay home. Let Dad rest." I can hear
her sigh. "Your sister had chorus again, right? She's a
soprano, isn't she?"

"Maybe, I'm not sure," I say. Is this *my* mother?

"I think so. And send Edward out for pizza, or whatever."

"I will."

"So I'll be home later; I'm going to wait for Dr. Sweeney
again."

"Mom!" I just want to say something.

"What is it?" I can imagine the expression on her face,
same as the picture. The rumpled, sad mouth.

"What do you want for dinner?" I say.

"Oh, I don't care. It doesn't matter." She hangs up.

What did I want to say? Maybe yes, it does. The phone
rings again.

"Hello," I answer.

"Same to you," Jane says.

"I was just going to call you . . ."

"Does that mean you can meet me?" she asks.

"End of the driveway," I say.

"When? Don't waste any time."

"What? Five minutes."

I write a note for Edward and Baby Teeth about Dad.

I wait five excruciating minutes before I walk outside.

"How's your dad?"

"Better, supposedly. For now."

"Oh good! Good good good!" she calls into the sky, but then she looks at me. "So what is it?"

"How do you know?" I mumble, already burning.

"Your face, V. What *is* it?"

Sometimes I hate when she calls me V. Again I can't look into her eyes. "I have to go," I say. It's not even close to dark. What am I doing?

Jane just looks at me.

"I'm nuts."

At least we laugh. "And nuts about you," whispers from my mouth, in a voice that surprises me, low and urgent.

Jane must be surprised too, because when she breathes, it's more like gasping, as if she's forgotten how to, or there's no air in the air when she does. After I say it,

I'm able, though I can't believe it, to look into her eyes.
It's like looking into the sun. Blinded.

"I have to go to the woods," I say, the words inching
into the air.
"What about me?" she says.
"You have to come too."

We begin to walk along without speaking. There's nothing else to say anyway. We know what we're going to
do. We're going to touch each other, and there're no
words for that. I can hardly breathe, and my new problem, every time I'm with Jane, is with me now. I struggle
to keep my legs moving, concentrating on lifting each
foot. But still I stumble, thinking she'll call it off any
minute. I think she trips a few times herself. It's like
we're drunk, the way we walk. Or dreaming. Dive, I
think to myself, or sink. I didn't forget.

I know a secret place in some woods near my house. I
go when I want to be alone, just to sit with the old
willow trees. Nobody has ever come along. It's hard to
get to, since there's no path, but not impossible. Only
for everyone else.

When we enter the woods, I walk in front of Jane since
I know the way. Hearing her steps behind mine, just
hearing her breathe, makes me dizzy. When we turn
into the thicket, her hand reaches out, but so barely it

nestles against the small of my back. Her touch streams along my spine, and a blazing chill rushes through me. I'm burning.

I don't know I'm running until we reach the clearing, the secret clearing that hides under those willows that must've been there forever, the way their branches spread through the air and reach the next tree. I don't know I'm running until I'm panting, like an animal, for God's sake, until she catches up with me and reaches for me and I say, I can't believe I have time to say, "I love you," before her mouth covers mine and my arms find a place around her, pull her against me and we fall, in one big moment, under the trees.

My hands rush over Jane as if they don't belong to me. Each time I touch her somewhere, and I have to touch her everywhere, she murmurs, the urgency of desire, the surrender to the hands that take us. My hands, so familiar, become strangers as they amble over her. The curves, the incredible softness as my hands ease beneath her shirt, the trembling breath.

And how simple it is, how natural. I know how to touch without ever having touched. I know without knowing. What have I been so afraid of? Not this part. The part when the sound of her voice plunges into my heart; the mention of her name like a dagger in my chest is what frightens me. So this is love? My hands ache with joy, wanting to linger around her lips, my arms ache from holding her so tightly, my chest aches, as if I am underwater, as if I have dived into a pool and rise, laggardly, unbreathing, to the surface. Suddenly, Jane slips her hand between my legs. I might dissolve in the deepening pleasure. So this is love.

d a n g e r

I watch my father breathe. That's all he does, so that's all I do. I can't imagine anything more mind-boggling than dying. Everyone, the one who is doing it, as well as the ones who are watching it, can do nothing else. We're at the hospital.

He can't move. He can't open his eyes. He's in a coma. A thick, transparent tube pumps blood into him; a skinny blue tube pumps protein. Another, a catheter, removes bodily waste. Nothing in his body is working except the tubes. And the respirator, which helps him breathe. The respirator mask covers most of his face.

It requires his entire body to breathe, and each time he exhales he looks like he's sinking. It sounds like he's sucking the air from the air. I catch myself holding my own breath as I watch him. Desperation, I guess. It's incredibly hard for him to breathe at all. So why should I?

My father's heart is electronically hooked up to a video monitor. Small white suction cups cover his chest, and wires connect to the monitor that blips green across the screen as his heart beats.

We watch it from around the bed. It's amazing that a few wires can turn a body inside out, make it possible to watch what's actually happening beneath the flesh. I look at the monitor, although I don't want to. I think the next blip will be the last. I look. I can't help it.

I wish my dad would wake up. This room is like ice. Even my hands are numb, I realize, as I smooth the blankets around my dad's feet. "Are you cold?" I say to Edward. But as he shakes his head, it's like a dream, as if he hasn't moved at all. I slip my hands around one of my father's. His hand is cold. Tears rise in my eyes. I'm talking, silently, to him. I'm saying, I will always remember you, and, all the stuff you told me about birds I won't forget, and I could even tell you what the flowers that are blooming now are called. I'm already remembering, isn't that something? I say, I love you, Daddy.

I step away. I wonder if he can hear me. If he can sense the pain that shovels into my side as I breathe. I finally say, I'm going to miss you. The tears are all over my face by the time I realize I already do.

Nobody is saying anything. As we surround the hospital bed, it's like we are a bunch of shoes, standing next to each other in a closet. We can fill our shoes, but that's all we can do. I guess I'm beginning to understand the silence. What is there to say anyway? There was so much blood; the blankets were so unbelievably heavy when I lifted them. How can he even be alive?

I'm beginning to see the silence for what it is, something finished in itself. It seems incredibly loud to me, like a hundred cars crashing into each other. Unbearably loud. And then it seems like the only place where there's any peace. It's in the silence that I wait for something. Wait for magic. For my dad to wake up.

| | | | | | | |

Back in elementary school, there was a space outside the school that was magic. Beyond the windows, at the end of the building where the red bricks suddenly curved in an arc—as if the building were turning into a castle—was a row of hedges whose always freshly cut tips just met the windowsills. The sills themselves were five feet from the ground, and the hedges ran, like soldiers, in a line from end to end. In the space between the hedges and the brick wall, a couple of feet or so, just big enough for me to fit, was the magic.

It happened when I stood there. Suddenly no one could see me. I was swooped into the invisible arms of sensation. Its grasp insisted that it was only I who lived. It was as if I had stepped directly into electricity. The sounds of my life were louder than the racket of all the sparrows in the world singing together at my side. All I had to do was lift my arm and it would roar through the air. When I scraped my heel, it rumbled across the dirt. The sounds came as if I were huge, stampeding, wild. I seemed to be instantly wider than the school itself and ten times its height. I was a giant, yet no one could see me. But I could see everything. And because I could see, because I was in the magic, there was nobody or nothing that I needed.

ı ı ı

But now I need somebody. Now the world seems full of everything but magic. Except for Jane. There's Jane. But with her, there's also confusion.

I recognize the fact, according to the world, I mean, that two girls having sex together, and not at least pretending one of them is a boy, is pretty unusual. What I don't understand is how it got to be that people still seem to think there's something wrong with it.

Even I think there's something wrong with it, and I don't know how that happened. Or I think I thought I did. But I don't. Not after having experienced it, the most natural thing in the world: love. Since I can't remember anything ever said out loud about the love part, I wonder how I arrived at the idea that it's wrong without even thinking about it. I guess that's where the danger is. In the things that aren't mentioned.

Is there something wrong with me? I thought I was a regular person. It feels like I don't know anymore. What it really feels like is that I'm finding out I never knew anything before.

Summer is only weeks away. Soon it will be so hot nobody will be able to breathe. I doubt we'll be going to the beach. We'll have to go to the hospital. To the Dairy Barn. We'll have to remain silent.

In the silence, we'll ask ourselves: Why is this happening? What does it mean? When dying gets to a certain excruciating point, does death become desirable? Please give my daddy some relief, I say into the air, before I know I have even thought it. How is that possible? I am silent.

deep

Late at night I am on fire. As I stay awake in the dark, so much more than air or breath or a smattering wind streams through me. So much more like fire.

The parts of me that fight each other burn behind my eyes like fists of glowing coals. Whether I believed Eileen was actually going to or not, she did call. "It's me, and I really think that after today—because everything with Lucky and Grant and the car accident is out in the open—we should keep talking, getting everything said and stop holding stuff back and just put it out there. So we can get on with our *lives*, don't you think, V?"

And I was, I really did listen to what she said and how impossible it seemed for her to go ahead and tell what it was she hadn't. I was envisioning her arms spreading and the fingers of her free hand opening, as she tried to say the truth out loud, the pale knuckles of the other hand as it gripped the telephone, and her eyes, which might be half shut with what I had finally figured out by then.

"So you're going out with Sullivan," I eventually said, because what else could it be? And why else would Sullivan try to wedge Lucky, like some rotten slab of discontent, between Eileen and me? If Sullivan could convince me that my friend had coldheart-edly taken off the day my dog got demolished, maybe I'd stop being her friend. He really wanted to hurt me, I figured. He did. It aches behind my eyes. Like fire.

And then, because Sullivan couldn't keep his secret to himself any longer, he'd finally tell *her* what had ac-tually happened that day, and because *I* was no longer talking to her, *she* wouldn't tell me. So not only would

Sullivan be able to lighten the baggage in his head by confessing—he'd also get the confidence of Eileen.

"Who told you that?" Eileen's voice shrilled in my ear. But nobody had told me—and that's why I'd been so confused. That's why Eileen had stopped calling, stopped talking, turned mean trying so hard to ignore me. So she was seeing Sullivan and was afraid to tell me. Was it as simple as that? That the more time passed without her telling me the worse it became? Or was it something else? What had Sullivan told her about *us?*

"Grant said he wouldn't talk to you until I had. Did he? He couldn't have"—Eileen answered herself—"he seems so afraid of you, V—it's Lucky, I guess. He really and deeply feels terrible, you know. I feel so bad. I didn't know what to say, really, about Grant, and then I thought I should wait to see if anything was really going on between Grant and me before I said something—you know how it is. And he asked me not to say anything too. But why would *he* care if *you* knew? But it wasn't only you—it was *everyone*, he said. He wanted to wait. But then everything started to happen —after Lucky got run over and then your dad was sick I didn't know what to do . . ."
"So do you love him? That's what matters . . ."

And I guess that was my voice, mouthing those words, but it seems so far, lagging, part of some other life.

The life that happens during the day when the light shines so bright I have to shield my eyes. I am on fire. My breath burns. Is this longing?

"What did he tell you about *us*, anyway?" I finally asked Eileen.

". . . That he kissed you."

"But that's not true—*I* kissed *him*. Just so you know— and only *once*," I said.

"You did? You never told me." The words slid quietly into my ears. She wanted to say them as little as I wanted to hear them.

"I'm sorry. I was too embarrassed, I think—one kiss and he disappeared. I don't know, I began to feel like I had done something *wrong*." I only thought he didn't like me. But all that evil was only *fear*—Sullivan wasn't trying to hurt me or my dog. It's just that he's afraid of me because *I* kissed *him*. Who would ever guess? I just didn't understand.

"What do you mean?"

I wish I knew what I meant. I watch the moon and ache with fire. I can barely understand.

But *so what* if I don't understand, all at once, everything that love and loss offer and demand in the same breath. It's the other life, late at night, that burns with a fury of questions behind my eyes, that will not stop asking, *what* is it that burns through me, *how* can the flame way deep in my chest beat so wildly in such absolute silence, *why* doesn't the fire die out?

Because I am alive

dust

rows are an interesting species of bird. They live in small groups. Up to a dozen survivors from the previous season form a group. Little crow families that will not have anything to do with other crow families when they're feeding. What they do is caw in their inimitable way, chasing members of other crow groups away from any food sources, as they dive and swoop. I've seen it myself.

I I I

What's so interesting about crows is that although they feed in the same territory every day, they fly up to fifty miles every night to roost with gaggles of other crows. How many in a gaggle anyway? In the case of crows, it's more than a few hundred families. All told, it's something like a hundred thousand crows gathered together. This is true.

If somebody stood and watched the crows fly from several different directions into the tops of, say, oak trees, and then saw the crows nestle into the branches around sunset, somebody'd notice that not a sound would escape from the branches after the hundred thousand crows settled in. Somebody'd notice that nobody else would even know they were there.

Since a hundred thousand things can be happening in the trees before somebody's very eyes without even being noticed, what about all the things that are happening *inside* somebody's head that people can't possibly see? What about the things that are happening inside the head of the person who's doing the looking? If people can't even see what's in front of them, how are they supposed to see what's inside if them? Even they want to more than anything else in the world? My father told me all about the crows. I remember.

I I I

I am standing in the hall at school, sort of paralyzed. I can't remember where I'm going. I don't know what time it is. My mother has called me at school. Somebody from the office came to my English class to tell me my mother was on the office telephone. I'm on my way to the office, but I'm standing in the hall. Sort of paralyzed.

I look out the hall window. There's nothing to see. At first, it is only green. The grass is green. And then some crows fly by.

Once I got a note at school. Now I get a telephone call. My mother is waiting for me on the phone. Why does she have to call anyway? I know what she's going to say. I don't know what words she will choose, but what does it matter? There are no words for it.

I don't care what time it is. It doesn't matter anyway. Things just happen and it doesn't matter what time it is. Somebody's entire world can change in a minute. In the instant a telephone rings. At the moment somebody looks out a window. A hundred thousand things can be happening as a crow flies by.

Knowing what time it is doesn't make any difference. Hearing my mother's voice on the telephone say "Your father died at eleven o'clock" isn't going to explain anything.

| | |

So why do I stand in the middle of a hallway staring at my watch? All my watch is going to tell is the time. It's not going to answer any other questions. It's not going to explain all the things I can't see. Or how it's possible that my daddy is suddenly, really, dreadfully dead.

So why do I stand here looking at my watch with my eyes so blurred with tears I can't even focus? I'm trying to see exactly when it was that my heart was broken.

dive

Hush, hush.
Reeling, spinning. My mind. My own home movie. My
father, his voice, the birds and flowers, the waves.
Burning, churning, weeping.

I don't imagine somebody gets to go backward very
often in life, but that's why my mind is reeling. Remembering.

| | |

So death makes an offering. Memories for the living.
Is that all? Hush.

I'm sitting in an upholstered chair. It is morosely blue.
My hands grip each arm of the chair. My feet, not quite
reaching the floor, sway slightly.

I am sitting at my father's wake. Beside me are the
remaining members of my family. There's a priest
standing in a corner of the room, near the coffin. He's
saying something, a prayer, I guess. I can't hear him.
It's as if I'm watching a silent movie. I have stopped
listening to anything but the bleating voice inside my
head. The small voice says, "My daddy died yesterday."

Eileen comes, takes one look at me, and says, "Let's
get a little air, come on, V, let's go."
We get to the hall, unsteady in our high heels.
"I can't believe how much my shoes hurt. Do yours?"
Eileen says.
"Like they belong to somebody else." My feet are
numb.

It's my mind that aches, reeling, spinning. My own
home movies, the shiny buttons, the Easter hats, my
father's grin. But it's all fading, the edges tattered. Like
those pictures in the basement, of my mother, fading.

Where is my mother? "I'll be right back," I say to Eileen.

"Hey, V." Eileen grabs my arm. "I'm really sorry about everything—and your dad, I mean, I don't know what to say."

Nobody ever does, and that's not what matters anyway. "Just be my friend." She looks like she might cry, but I can't really tell. My own eyes are all blurred.

I wander around the room. I see my brother, standing in the front by the coffin. When I'm ready, I say to myself. But I don't see my mother or Baby Teeth. Where's Eileen? Sitting on a chair, shoe in hand, she rubs her ankle.

"Too much leaning," she says. "Either I'm too tall for heels, or I'm just no good at this woman stuff." She wipes her eyes and smiles. "Anything else you want to tell me?"

I smile in return and sit next to her. "I was wondering about that hat of yours . . ."

She laughs. "It was a present, that's why."

"That's why what?"

"You hate it as much as I do. From Grant—it's the thought that counts, don't forget."

"Anything you say." We laugh.

I'm looking at Eileen without knowing how to say what I need to tell her about Jane.

"Just be my friend too, okay?" she says. What that means to me is that somebody tells the truth.

I take a breath and feel almost giddy as I realize it's only air, not fire. "I'm trying," I say. "So where is he?"

"Outside, I think. He dropped me off."

I stand.

"Where are you going?" Eileen asks.

I look around the room again. Baby Teeth and my mother appear, smiling, in the doorway.

I walk toward them. So much seems to be happening.

I exhale, wondering what is real. "What is it?"

"Daddy said, when I forgot is when they would." Baby Teeth wiggles a tooth. "Do you want to see?"

Maybe people don't really die at all, my mind says. Hush. "I knew I felt magic around—I should've known it was you. Dad's right, I guess," I say as I kneel and embrace my sister.

When I stand, I begin to reach for my mother. What separates us is the darkness in her eyes. I can't change that. I wonder if *anyone* can forgive themselves.

I turn, my own eyes burning. Let the wind in, my mind says.

"Where are you going?" Eileen calls. "You still haven't answered me."

I will, and as I approach the door, I see Jane through the window, her hands filled with flowers. How I wish

I could say without words what I experience. Because my eyes, on fire, see so much more than I understand.

You know when you go to sleep and you have hopes? Baby Teeth said that a long time ago. I guess you can have them when you're awake too. Because, surrounded by all these people, and the endlessness of everything I already remember, I am on fire. Unbelievably dreamy with hopes. And I wish I could feel this way forever.